MY WOLFY WEDDING

Peculiar Mysteries Book 8

RENEE GEORGE

Barkside of the Moon Press

My Wolfy Wedding

Peculiar Mysteries Book 8

Cover Art: Renee George

Print Date: 12/31/2018

ISBN: 978-1-947177-26-0

ACKNOWLEDGMENTS

I have to thank Robbin Clubb, the island of Bonaire where I finished writing the story, and my husband for not hassling me for turning our vacation into a work vacation.

Chav and Billy Bob are finally getting the wedding they deserve and I can't wait for you all to read it!

I need to thank Renee's Rebels for continuing to support my work, read it, promote it, and love it. You all are ROCK STARS!

I also want to thank the town of Peculiar, whose name I borrowed then used my creative fiction license to relocated them from the north of Missouri to down south in the Ozarks, for giving me a kick ass place to start. Stay peculiar, Peculiar!

And finally, I have to give many, many thanks to hot black coffee. You got me there!

Billy Bob Smith and Chavvah Trimmel cordially request the honor of your presence on their happy (disastrous) day. To celebrate (survive) their union on Friday, the Twenty-First of December, Two Thousand Eighteen at Four-Twenty-Three p.m.

Destination: Peculiar, Missouri.

The only thing Chavvah wants more than to marry Billy Bob is to have his baby, but since that ship has sailed thanks to prior trauma, she's happy just to get him down the aisle. The date is set for the Winter Solstice, marking the longest night of year, but a challenge from an unexpected guest, is turning her special day into a fight-club nightmare. And after having postponed the wedding twice already, Chav is starting to think fate hates her guts.

On top of that, there are almost forty werewolves camped out on Billy Bob's property, claiming that Chav and Billy Bob are their new leaders. But when Chav tries to get her spirit guide, Brother Wolf, to cough up answers, he ignores her. Even worse, the silent deity is sending her BFF Sunny visions that are taking a physical toll on her human friend's all too frail body.

Throw in Billy Bob's manipulative father, Chav's pushy mother, and other surprise guests, these two furry lovebirds may never make it to "I do!"

For my husband,
You have given me a lifetime of At Lasts,
and I love you.

CHAPTER ONE

*D*ecember *19ᵗʰ, Two days before my wedding date...*

"The weather man is calling for mild temperatures this entire week," Sunny said. "High forties to mid
fifties. It looks like you're going to have an unseasonably
warm winter nuptial, Chav. Isn't that good news?" She
clapped her hands and danced around me. Dawn and
Jude, my adorable nephew and niece, giggled at their
mother's antics.

"I don't need a white wedding," I told her. Though I really
wanted one. The idea of getting married under fairy lights
in a blanket of snow, against the contrast of red roses and
carnations made my inner princess squee. Doc had agreed
to wear a white tux, but I'd had to suffer through a little
razzing from all my friends about how girly I was getting.
Frankly, I didn't give a crap. I was marrying the wolf of my
dreams in less than a week. Nothing and no one was going
to put a damper on my great mood.

My phone, sitting on the counter near the coffee pot, beeped. I walked over and looked down at the text.

"No," I said, unable to keep the horror from my tone.

"What is it?" Sunny asked.

I held up the phone for her to see. She gasped.

I seconded that emotion.

The text was from my mother, and it only contained three words. *On my way.* I cast an accusatory glance at Sunny. "Who told her?"

"Not me." Her expression mirrored my horror. "Your mother has a way of ruining a perfectly good wedding."

"You mean, she has a way of trying to put an end to a perfectly good wedding." She wasn't happy about my engagement to Billy Bob Smith, a pure lycanthrope, and the only one of his kind in this area. "She still thinks that werewolves are violent rogues who have no self-control."

Sunny snorted. "I've been in the other room when you two are having sex. I don't think she's wrong about that self-control thing."

I laughed. "Well, he's certainly not violent."

Sunny nodded. "Not any more than anybody else in this town."

"Besides, I can shift into a wolf now, so I don't understand what her deal is. We're part-flippin-werewolf." Recently I'd discovered I could shift into either wolf or coyote depending on my mood. According to Billy Bob, I was one of a kind. I shook my head as I pictured my mother's reaction to the news of my tri-nature, and how my ancestral heritage made all the lycanthrope bigotry complete and utter bullshit. "The family vendetta was a complete lie. Why can't she just give it up?"

"I've got no answers, Chav. I gave her two grandchildren, and, still, she barely tolerates me."

"Mom doesn't hate you."

Sunny snorted again.

"Well, not as much as she hates Billy Bob."

"That's probably true. She even tried to get me to side with her at Thanksgiving."

I raised my brow at her. "You ate Thanksgiving with me."

"On the phone," she confessed.

"Oh."

"Don't worry. I totally had your back. I told her that there wasn't enough BFF ju-ju in this world that could pry your legs from around that man's waist."

"Sunny!" My face flamed with heat. "You didn't."

She shrugged. "I might not have used those exact words, but something to that effect. As the saying goes, the va-jay-jay wants what the va-jay-jay wants."

"That's not how the saying goes." A knock at the door rescued me from the deteriorating conversation.

Sunny smiled. "That's probably her now."

I groaned. "Damn it." I left Sunny, who wasn't eager to see my mom either, in the kitchen as I walked through the living room to the front door. I braced myself for the ill-wind blowing in and opened the door just as another knock occurred.

My mother was not on the others side of the door. Instead, an extremely tall, lanky gentleman with short silver hair, gray-blue eyes, and golden skin. There were fine lines around his eyes that marked him as an elder.

"Can I help you?"

"Is William home?"

"Who?"

The man looked surprised. "William Smith."

"Billy Bob?"

The guy nodded, his expression full of disapproval. "Yes, him."

"He's not home right now." Normally, Billy Bob worked at the clinic during the daytime hours. Today, however, he was getting fitted for his tux, along with his best men Brady Corman, Babe, and Ed Thompson. "Can I give him a message?"

The man hemmed and hawed for a moment then finally

said, "Yes." He cast me a steely stare. "Tell him his father is in town, and I'd like to see him at his earliest convenience."

I returned a suspicious gaze. "Does he know how to contact you?"

The man pulled his wallet from his back pocket and produced a card. William Robert Smith, Sr. Smith Contractors, LLC, and a business number along with a mobile phone number. Mister Smith handed me the card and said, "He can call me on my cell phone."

I took the card and saluted with it. "I'll give him the message."

"Can I ask you a question?"

I shrugged. "Sure."

"Who are you?"

I knew enough not to be hurt that Billy Bob's dad had no idea who I was or what I meant to his son. The doc told me once he hadn't spoken to his father in over fifteen years. He hadn't elaborated, and I hadn't pried. Now, as I studied the man, who really didn't look much like my mate at all, I kind of wished I would have—pried, that is. "I'm his...girlfriend," I finally said. Not a lie, but not the whole truth. I didn't know if Billy Bob wanted his dad crashing our festivities. I know I sure didn't want my mom there.

"Is this his house or yours?" he asked.

"That's two questions." I smiled to soften my words.

"It is," he agreed. "My apologies. Please give the message to William. Tell him I don't like to be kept waiting."

And Doc doesn't like to be bossed. I crossed my arms as irritation replaced my curiosity. It was no wonder Billy Bob left home and never looked back.

"Chav?" Sunny asked when she walked into the living room. "Are you okay?"

William Smith turned his gaze to my friend. His eyes were that of a pure predator. "She's human." Even though he was staring at her, he addressed me. His accusation surprised me because there wasn't any way to tell if someone was therian or human based on looking at them or even by scent. "I thought this place was a therianthrope haven." The little growl in his voice raised the hairs on the back of my neck.

His demeanor pushed my animal to the surface, and I think William was a surprised as me to find it was wolf, not coyote, who challenged him.

"There are no other lycanthropes in this territory. What tribe are you from?" His interest had turned back to me and away from Sunny.

I let out a slow breath forcing my wolf to retreat. "I'll let the doc know you stopped by." Since he still stood just outside on the porch, I took a step forward, my hand on the door, closing it between us. I turned to Sunny.

She ran a hand through her short, blonde hair. "Looks like your mom isn't the only parental wedding crasher. Mister Smith seems like a real sweetheart."

I walked over to window and peeked behind the curtain. A truck pulled back up then took off down the driveway toward the one road in and out of town.

"I've got a bad feeling about that one."

Sunny put her hand on my shoulder. "Hey, you can't have the psychic gig. It's the only thing I got going for me. You know, aside from saggy milk sacks and crow's feet."

"There's always plastic surgery. I hear they're doing amazing things with stem cell therapy. You don't even have to go under a knife for that."

"Mean," Sunny said. Her lower lip jutted in a fake pout. "Seriously though, does that stem cell stuff work, because..."

"Oh, stop it. You're beautiful. And I have it on good authority that your husband adores you just the way you are."

"I know. I'm just working on a contingency plan. You know, for the future." Sunny wrapped her arms around me, and for a human, she gave the most spine crushing hugs of anyone I'd ever met.

Frankly, it was just what I needed. "I don't know what I'd do without you."

"Good thing you don't have to. You're stuck with me,

darling." She unclenched her arms from around me. "I better go though. Michele Thompson has a date tonight, and I promised I'd be home before four so she could get cleaned up for it."

"Jo Jo?" I asked. Jo Jo Corman, a twenty-one-year-old coyote shifter who'd been working for Sunny and me at Sunny's Outlook for nearly three years had a real thing for Michele. They'd dated before, but the girl could be fickle.

"I didn't ask, and she didn't volunteer," Sunny said. "But Jo Jo finally shaved the scruff off his face and got a new haircut yesterday." She picked up her purse and gave me another quick hug. "I'll see you tonight."

CHAPTER TWO

The uneasiness of William Smith's visit hadn't waned. Every time I thought about the smug, domineering wolf, my own wolf would surface. So, when Billy Bob walked through the door, another instinct all together took over me. I draped my arms around his neck and raised up on my toes to meet his lower face in a kiss that steamed the windows in the living room.

Hot damn, that man curled my toes.

His hands kneaded their way down my back until his palms cupped my ass, and he lifted me up. I crawled up his torso, locking my feet behind his thighs, and sunk deeper into the kiss.

Billy Bob's chest rumbled as he turned and pushed me up against the wall, his hands roaming like someone trying to find a light switch in the dark.

"Yowza," he growled. "Hello, beautiful." He cupped the

back of my neck. "I've missed you, too." His gray eyes sparkled with dark desire.

I tugged his shirt up and over his head. "Too many clothes," I told him. The skin on his wide chest shivered under my fingertips. I tweaked his nipple and grinned.

He smiled. "How'd I get so lucky?"

"I'm the--" The doorbell chimed before I could finish my sentence, and a second later my mother pushed her way inside.

"I texted you," she said with a tone full of accusation.

Cripes. Me up against the wall, riding my half-naked fiancé was not how I wanted to greet my mom. Frankly, not having to greet her at all would have been preferable.

"I forgot," I said, easing myself off of Billy Bob while he grabbed his shirt from the floor and quickly put it back on.

"Hello, Celia," my mate said with more courtesy than Mom deserved. "To what do we owe the pleasure of your company."

Mom took her jacket off and hung it on the coat rack to the right of the door. She placed her purse on the ground and tucked her gloves into one of the folds. She looked at me, her sour expression full of disapproval. After she made sure I got the message, she turned her gaze to Billy Bob. "My only daughter is getting married in two days. Did you really think I would stay away?"

"Given your feelings about who I'm marrying, I'd hoped you would stay away," I said. I crossed my arms over my chest partly to show my indignation, but mostly to hide my pre-coitus erect nipples.

Billy Bob filled in the space next to me but didn't try to mediate the tension between me and my contentious parent. I found that most men wanted to solve a woman's problems, even when she didn't ask for or want a solution. I loved Doc all the more for not trying to "fix" things.

Mom sighed. "You don't have to be so..."

"Honest," I said.

She narrowed her brow at me. "I raised you to be polite."

I felt a twinge of something resembling guilt. God, I hated how my mom could turn me into the teenage version of myself. "Mom, why are you really here?"

"I told you. I am here for your wedding."

"But you—"

She held up a hand to silence me. "I'm not going to miss my only daughter's walk down the aisle, and neither is your father. He'll be joining us Friday after he gets off work."

My dad was a safety specialist for a manufacturer in Kansas City. My whole life he'd worked at the same plant, eight to five, Monday through Friday, except for vacation weeks. "You can't be here if you can't be civil."

"Don't worry. I'm going to stay with your brother."

I caught myself before the uptick at the corner of my mouth turned into a full-blown grin. "You're going to torture Sunny instead of me? I couldn't ask for a better wedding gift."

"Don't be fresh, girl," Mom snapped. "Pretty is as pretty does, and right now, you are not very attractive."

My stoic mate rumbled with a suppressed growl. I reached over and took his hand. "Wolves are very protective." My comment was a childish dig on my mother's prejudices. I'd been raised on a healthy diet of lycanthropy hate. "And loyal," I added.

"Yes, yes," my mom said dismissively. "I get it. I was wrong. Werewolves are not the evil savages my mother taught me to believe, but you have to understand that I can't undo eighty years of history overnight."

"Mom, what are you doing here? Really?"

"I'm trying to make things right." Her face was a reflection of the fight going on inside her, a weird combination of pride and remorse. "I'm trying to apologize."

"For the love of Pete." I threw up my hands. "If you want to apologize then do it. It's easy, just say, I'm sorry."

"I accept your apology," she said.

"Mom!"

"I'm joking." She flashed a smile my way.

Billy Bob cross the room to Mom faster than I could stop him. I gasped as he raised his arms...and hugged her. What?

My mother stiffened for a moment, her balled up fists clenched by her sides. I held my breath waiting for her head to explode.

Then I heard it, a light tinkle of laughter. I let out a shaky exhalation and smiled as Mom's arms rose up and wrapped Billy Bob's waist. After a few seconds, they parted, both of them smiling.

I pursed my lips for a moment then said, "You good?"

Mom nodded. "Yep. And wow, my soon to be son-in-law smells really nice."

I laughed. "He really does." Billy Bob was back at my side now, his hand in mine once again. I gave his fingers a squeeze of thanks.

"I'll let you two have a minute or two alone. It'll give me a chance to catch up on some work in the clinic."

Crap. I hadn't told him about his dad showing up out of the blue. He needed to know, but it wasn't the kind of bomb I wanted to drop in front of my mom. Especially, since his dad seemed exactly like the kind of wolf mom had warned us about.

"Okay," I said, instead of vomiting my news, "I'll call you when it's time for dinner."

"You staying for supper, Celia?" Billy Bob asked.

"I appreciate the offer, but I told Babe I'd eat with him and Sunny tonight."

Is it bad that I wiped the metaphorical sweat from my brow? I mean, I was happy to mend fences with my mom, but I wasn't sure I wanted to spend the whole evening with her. The woman could be difficult even under the best the conditions. She would find a way to criticize my food, my hair, my skin, my clothes, the decor in the house, and whatever else popped into her head. There was a reason I moved to California as soon as I was old enough to go. It was far, far away from Kansas City and Celia Trimmel.

"That's too bad, but if you've made other plans, I totally understand."

Mom rifled through her purse and pulled out her phone. "You know what, I'm just going to call your brother and tell him that my plans have change. I'd love to stay for dinner."

I gave Billy Bob a quick look that I hoped conveyed just how unlucky he was going to get tonight then smiled at Mom. "Great. The more the merrier."

I'D PLANNED fried pork chops for dinner, but since I wasn't about to do dinner with mom without a buffer, I changed it to eggplant parmesan to accommodate Sunny's psychic aversion to meat. Nothing ruined a dinner party like a seizure inducing vision of animal slaughter. I set the table for five in the rarely-used formal dining room. I preferred eating dinner on the couch snuggled up next to the doc but desperate times and all that.

"Coming!" I shouted when the doorbell rang. When I flung the door back, it wasn't Sunny and Babe on the other side, it was, once again, William Smith, Sr.

With a groan, I slammed the door shut between us. "Oh, shit." I took a deep breath, debating whether or not to open the door again or treat him like I would a vacuum salesman, and turn off all the lights and pretend I wasn't home.

"Where's your brother?" Mom asked. She looked around the living room. "Wasn't that him and Sunny at the door?"

"Uhm..."

Knock. Knock. Knock.

"Chav?" Mom made a shooing motion with her hands. "Answer the door."

"No." I slapped my hand over my mouth.

Mom strolled past me. "What in the world has gotten into you, girl?" She flung the door open before I could stop her.

William Smith narrowed his gray gaze on my mother. "Who are you?"

My mom's back stiffened. "Who are you?"

He leaned in toward Mom and took a deep inhalation. "I

don't have to answer to a coyote." He spat out the last word as if it were a bad taste in his mouth.

Jesus, this dude's sense of smell was like a blood hound, and frankly, I took exception to his disdain. A growl rumbled in my chest.

William's gray eyes, stormy with anger, shifted in my direction. "That's the second time you shut the door in my face. Are you sure you want to challenge me?"

"When you invited us for dinner, I had no idea asshole was on the menu," Sunny said as she strolled in the front door behind William.

Babe, crating my adorable nephew and niece in his arms, followed her past the fuming werewolf. "What is going on now?" he said resignedly. "And am I going to have to write a report for the Tri-State Council?"

Sunny put her industrial sized diaper bag down and stood next to me to face William, her arms crossed over her chest in an act of defiance. "I'd say Billy Bob's daddy has pissed off a wolf spirit." She shrugged. "If I had to guess."

William glared at my BFF, a snarl of contempt on his lips. "Shut up, human."

Both Babe and Billy Bob growled.

"What do you want, Father?" Billy Bob asked. "Why are you here?" That question was getting asked a lot today.

"I'm here because you didn't call me."

"When was I supposed to call you?"

"I told your coyote-bitch this afternoon—"

I looked guiltily at Billy Bob, since I hadn't told him about the earlier visit, but he hadn't taken his eyes off his dad to look my way.

"Chavvah is no one's bitch," Sunny said.

Actually, since a female coyote-wolf is technically a bitch, I was less offended than my enraged friend. "It's better than being a piece of dog shit," I said.

Sunny linked her arm in mine in a show of solidarity.

"This is the last time I'll ask you," Billy Bob said to his dad. "What do you want?"

"I want to know why you are suddenly interested in taking my position in our tribe? Why after all these years?"

"I have no idea what you're talking about, old man. I never wanted your position. Why do you think I left—"

"Ran away," his father sniped.

"Whatever you want to believe," Billy Bob said, his voice growing eerily quiet with anger. "Believe this. I am not interested in pack politics. Never have been."

"Wait a minute," Sunny said. "Lycanthropes live in packs? How did I not know this?"

The way Billy Bob had explained it, lycanthropes didn't

really live in packs. They considered themselves more like a community, a tribe, held together by ancestral blood. His grandfather had been the shaman of their tribe, and he'd been grooming the doc to take over as spiritual leader. I knew his grandfather had passed away but he'd never explained why he hadn't stayed with his people. Since it seemed like a painful subject for my guy, I'd let it go. Now, I wished I would have pressed a little because I was completely lost in this conversation.

I pinched Sunny's arm. "Not now."

"All right," she said, tugging her arm away. "Ix-nay on the ack-pay." She rubbed where I'd pinched. "And ow."

"Sorry."

She gave me a sympathetic nod. "I'll forgive you because I know what it's like to have a lunatic for an in-law."

"Hey!" Mom snapped.

Sunny gave me a sly smile then nodded toward Billy Bob and his dad, who both looked like they were about to go twelve rounds without gloves.

A loud *beep, beep, beep*! Startled everyone in the room.

"What in the hell is that?" Sunny asked as the beeping continued in a loud, grating high pitched tone.

The scent of burnt eggplant wafted into the living room. "Damn it! It's the smoke detectors!"

"Sunny and I will handle it," my mom said. The beeping

continued. "You stay and referee the dominant wolf pissing contest."

Before I could respond to her uncharacteristic language, she'd grabbed Sunny by the hand and the two of them headed toward the kitchen. Even over the alarm, I could hear Sunny cussing, my mom fussing, the sound of what I suspected was my broom whacking plastic before the smoke detector was silenced.

"Got it!" Sunny yelled from the other room. "Man, it's smoky as hell in here."

With one crisis averted, I turned my attention back to my honey and his papa wolf. "William, I think it's time for you to leave our home." When he gave me another challenging stare, Brother Wolf decided to intervene. "You will leave, *servus*," he commanded with my voice.

"I am not your servant," William said, but he averted his gaze.

I felt satisfaction from Brother Wolf.

Aren't you being a little petty? I asked the spirit.

I almost expected him to declare that William had started it first, but Brother Wolf was disappointingly quiet.

"What makes you think that Billy Bob," William winced when I used the nickname, "wants to suddenly take your pack from you?"

The older wolf shifter growled. "Because he does."

"Based on what evidence?"

"Based on the fact that half my town is camped on the outskirts of Peculiar, waiting to be invited in."

"That's impossible," I said.

"We didn't invite any wolves here," Billy Bob added.

About that... Brother Wolf muttered.

"Oh boy."

"What?" Billy Bob asked.

"Brother Wolf," I said.

"Hokum," William muttered.

Sunny staggered into the living room, her nose bleeding, while Mom propped her up, and did a semi-decent imitation of Ricky Ricardo when she said, "Oh, Brother Wo-olf. You have some *splainin'* to do."

CHAPTER THREE

*B*lood dripped down Sunny's lip, her skin pale as her hands trembled. Babe had his arm around her, propping her up. Billy Bob, who was the kind of guy who kept a handkerchief on him at all times, gave his to Sunny, and she dabbed at her nose.

"Are you all right?" I cast an accusing look at my mother. "Did mom punch you in the nose?"

"Don't be ridiculous, Chavvah," Mom said. "One minute she was pulling the casserole out of the oven, and the next, she was flopping on the floor. I'm assuming she had one of her vision-thingies." Mom said vision the same way some people say cancer, in a hushed tone while wincing at the prospect. She wagged her finger at Sunny. "Pinch the nose, dear, don't dab."

"And tilt your head forward a little," said Billy Bob. "That way you know when the bleeding stops, and it's not just running down the back of your throat instead of out your nose."

Mom nodded, and it was weird seeing her and Doc agree on something.

"What did you see?" I asked Sunny. She'd had visions about Brother Wolf before, but only when she'd been focused on me, not burnt dinner.

"Visions?" William scoffed. "More hokum! It figures you'd be mixed up in this kind of nonsense," he said to Billy Bob. "The worst thing I ever did was let you go live with your grandfather."

"It's not hokum, Father. Just because you never had the gift for spirit talking doesn't mean it isn't real," Doc growled. "And as I recall, you didn't let me go. I chose to apprentice with him."

His dad's face reddened, but before William could respond, Sunny chimed in, "I saw a shadow man with dark swirly, sparkly eyes," she glanced toward me first then Billy Bob. "And it looked like he was scrolling through images like Jo Jo does with social media on his phone. He didn't look happy. I think it was Brother Wolf, or one of his kind. The field he was in reminded me of the time I hitched a ride with Chav to the *aether*.

"Brother Wolf doesn't exist. He's a fairytale." William balled his fingers into fists. "This is the kind of spiritual hoodoo that keep lycanthropes from moving forward.

When are you going to learn that Brother Wolf only exists in your head?"

"Tell dat to him when he turns Chavvah into a monster wolf, large enough to bite your head off." Sunny stuck her tongue out at the crotchety alpha wolf and blood dripped down from under the hanky. "Oops." She pinched her nostrils harder. "Well, dis sucks," she said.

"This is nonsense," William said. "And I don't have time for it."

"Then go home, Father," Billy Bob said.

"Not without my wolves."

"They are where they are meant to be," Sunny said ominously. "That was in the vision. Though it was more an idea than a visual."

Mom shook her head. "Land sakes, your visions are as clear as mud."

Before I could intercede on Sunny's behalf, Babe said, "Leave her alone, Mom." He put his arm around Sunny.

I'd known my bestie long enough to take her psychic abilities seriously, even if they weren't always transparent in meaning. "It's important, whatever it means."

"Are you all right, darling?" Babe's frown and furrowed brow reflected his worry for his fragile and all too human wife—which made me worry. Sunny was older than Babe and aging more rapidly. She was also susceptible to a lot more illnesses than therianthropes. She'd confided to me several months back that she'd rather have something like a heart attack take her out before putting Babe through the agony of watching her die of old age. I'd smacked her shoulder, hard, and told her to stop being stupid. But I understood her concern. We'd both loved Highlander, the original movie, not the television series, but seeing Connor MacLeod watch his wife Heather wither with age and die in his arms was the ultimate heartbreak.

Sunny looked at me then glanced away. "That one was a doozy. That's the third time in three days that I've had a vision knock me for a loop. They feel like they're getting stronger."

"What happened in the first two?" When she didn't answer right away, I asked. "Was it about me?"

She shook her head then nodded once. "I don't know. I thought the first one was a dream, though I've never had a dream drive me to my knees before."

Babel narrowed his gaze on her. "You didn't tell me about that."

She gave me a sidelong look. "I saw seven couples, each with a baby."

My heart skipped a beat.

Sunny met my gaze then looked down and shook her head. "Each child and parent turned into a wolves and cubs respectively."

The same night she'd confessed her age-worry, I'd

confessed my baby-woes. Billy Bob had told me my uterus had been too damaged during my kidnapping to ever conceive, and I'd gone to see an ob/gyn in St. Louis, who had confirmed his diagnosis. I'd wanted more than anything to have his child, and that would never happen.

William Smith scoffed, snapping me out of my self-pitying moment. "That's impossible."

Sunny shrugged, then shook the bloody handkerchief at the crotchety werewolf. "I see what I see. It could have been the past. I have a tendency toward really unhelpful visions of the past, present, and future. I didn't see anything to indicate time or place. Technology is a good indication sometimes, like smart phones are the present, flip phones the past, touch tone the way past, rotary the way, way past."

Babel took her hand and pressed it back to her nose.

"I remember rotary phones," Billy Bob said.

"Old man," Sunny joked, but I didn't laugh. My best friend was having visions that involved werewolves, and she was getting the metaphysical shit beaten out of her in the process. I was too worried to laugh.

Brother Wolf, I summoned. I wanted more explanation, but the spirit guardian had gone radio silent on me. *Come out, come out where ever you are. I swear, if you're sending these visions to Sunny and she gets hurt in the receiving I will make you pay.* It was mostly an empty threat. There wasn't much I could do to a god-like entity that didn't recognize the flow of time and borrowed my body like a cheap suit every time he wanted to make an appearance. I shook my head at Billy Bob when he raised a brow at me. "Brother Wolf might know what's going on, but he isn't talking."

My soon to be father-in-law paced the room full of what can only be described as anxious rage. "It has to be the past."

"Why don't you just order your people to go home?" Billy Bob asked his dad. "You are their leader the last time I checked." He gave me a side glance then shifted his gaze back to William. "You are still the leader, right?"

The older lycanthrope shifted uncomfortably. "It's been a hard couple of years."

Billy Bob crossed his arms. "And that means?"

"There hasn't been a new lycanthrope born in twenty-one years."

"In the entire town?"

"Yes." William nodded. "I don't know if it's happening in other places, but there hasn't been any new births in over two decades in White Rock." He rubbed his callused hand over his face. "It's hard to keep a community together when old members die off and there are no young to replace them."

Billy Bob's naturally tan skin paled. "I don't believe you."

"I told you he wouldn't be any help," a soft, feminine voice said from the open doorway. A tall woman with silvery-white hair and silver eyes stood with her arms crossed, staring hard at Doc. "He's a traitor to our kind."

"Who are you?" I asked.

Billy Bob face had hardened at the sight of her.

I looked at him. "Do you know who she is?" She looked young, too young for her to have been someone he grew up with, but an overwhelming sense of foreboding threatened to swallow me up from the inside out.

"I do not," Billy Bob ground out through clenched teeth.

I felt Sunny's hand on my shoulder. I turned to find my friend giving me a consolatory look. "Would someone tell me what the hell is going on, and who this girl is?"

"She's the last born in our tribe," William said. "Her mother was Roberta Windsong."

Billy Bob's voice grew low and dangerous. "You said Robbie was dead."

"She is dead," the woman said. "She died giving birth." She put her hands on her hips. "To me."

"No," Billy Bob said.

"You'd run off to start your medical internship in another state, son," his dad said. "Robbie didn't want you to come back to her because she was pregnant. She wanted you to come back for her because you wanted her, so she made me promise not to tell you."

Lightning fast, Billy Bob had his father shoved up against the far wall. "You're lying. She would have told me."

"You can tell if I'm lying, boy." His dad looked at him with a stare that almost made my own wolf want to bow, but Billy Bob didn't even blink. After a few seconds, his Dad was the one to first avert his gaze.

The girl seemed surprised at William's submissive gesture, so much so, she rushed to him, trying to push Billy Bob away from the older wolf. "Get off of him!"

The doc remained unmovable for a few more seconds, before he gave his father a final shove then walked to the couch and sat down on the arm rest.

I felt my world spinning around me. Was this really happening? Billy Bob had a child--with another woman. Babe came around the other side of me, as he and Sunny huddled to me for comfort. How was I supposed to react to this? Billy Bob was in his fifties. Of course, he'd had a life before me, but I'd never imagined...

"You have a daughter," I said, my voice strained and quiet. I summoned strength where I could find it, from my best friend and my brother. I made myself stand tall and cleared my throat, speaking loudly and with as much geniality as I could muster. "Doc, you have a daughter. You might not have known about her before, but now you do. She is blood, and that makes her family."

I crossed the room to the surprised silver-haired beauty.

Hugging her was more than I was ready for, so I thrust out my hand instead as a peace offering. "Hi, I'm Chav."

The girl raised a brow at me. "You are not wolf," she said.

"Rudeness runs in the family," I heard Sunny say.

The girl leaned forward then and inhaled my scent deeply. "Yet, you smell like home."

"Why didn't you tell me about her after Robbie died?" Billy Bob asked his dad.

"What was the point?"

Doc growled then looked at the girl. "What's your name?"

"Why do you care now?" she asked, defiance strong in her voice. "Let's go, father," she said to William.

Billy Bob flinched. "You are not his daughter."

"I didn't want you to find out about her like this," William said.

Billy Bob chuckled but it wasn't because he was happy. "You were right. I can tell when you're lying. You hoped the girl would throw me and somehow give you some leverage over me. You always were a manipulative bastard."

"He was there for me when you weren't," the girl said.

"Let's go, Etta," William said. "There's no talking to him when he gets like this."

"Etta?" Billy Bob stood up. "You named her after Mom?"

"Robbie gave her the name," William said, and I could see it struck another blow for Billy Bob. "She loved you and our tribe more than you ever did."

Before my guy could launch himself at his father again, I put myself between them. "There has been a lot of information revealed tonight that needs to be digested." Unlike my ruined dinner. "Why don't you two comeback tomorrow morning for breakfast when Doc has had a moment to think."

"Besides," Sunny said. "This werewolf dick-swinging contest is giving me a headache."

"Lycanthropes," William said.

"Huh?"

"We don't like to be called werewolves. It's a human construct."

"Oooo," she wiggled her fingers. "Wouldn't want to be labeled."

I gave my friend a look of warning then turned my attention back to our guests. "Tomorrow morning," I told William and Etta. "Say nine a. m.."

"Nine a.m.," William repeated. "Then we'll discuss how my son is going to make things right with the tribe, so we can *all* go home."

I didn't like the way he'd said, *all*, but I let it slide for the moment. "Great." I walked them to the door and closed it behind them. After, I stared at Sunny. "What was the second vision about."

She gave me a sheepish glance. "There was a girl with silver hair. How in the world could I know it was the doc's kid? Seriously?"

"Why didn't you tell me? You always tell me when you have a psychic episode, but now that you're injuring your-self with them and they seem to be about my life, you're mum? What the heck, Sunny?"

"She had blood on her hands," Sunny said. "Lots of it."

"What else?" Billy Bob asked.

"That's all," Sunny said. "Oh, she was crying. Blood and crying." Defensively, she added, "Up until a few minutes ago, I didn't think she was real. I mean, she's basically the female version of Billy Bob, and unless he was planning to change genders..." She raised her hands, palms up. "I didn't think she was real. I thought she was symbolic, but I wasn't sure what she was symbolic for. I wanted to tell you, Chav." Sunny handed the handkerchief to Babel, her nose bleed finally stopped. She stood up and walked over to me. "It's your wedding week. I didn't want to ruin anything for you. This is supposed to be the most special time of your life."

I gave her a sour look. "It's been special, all right."

Billy Bob tried to take my hand, but I pulled away. I wasn't mad at him. Not really. But I wasn't ready to talk to him, yet. I needed some time to think about what had just happened. He had a daughter. He'd loved before me. Had he been ready to marry this Robbie before she died? Did it matter? Should it?

"Chav," he said, tone pinched and worried.

"I'm okay," I told him. I forced myself to meet his gaze.

"I can tell when you're lying, too," he said.

"Just this once," I said softly, "let's pretend you can't."

He wasn't okay, either. Learning he had a child he never knew existed had to be rocking him to his core. And worst of all, she seemed to hate him. I wanted to comfort him and tell him we would get through this, but right now, I was facing my own demons. I could never give him a baby, but someone had, and he'd been robbed of seeing his child grow up the same way I'd been robbed of ever conceiving.

I glanced at Sunny, Babe, and my mom. "I think you all should go." Before Sunny or my mom could protest, I added, "We'll catch up tomorrow. I promise."

After they left, Billy Bob said, "Are we okay?"

"Yes," I said and hoped like hell he wouldn't call me out for another lie.

CHAPTER FOUR

*W*e'd cleaned the kitchen together in mutually agreed silence. I dried the dishes while Doc fixed the smoke detector and placed it back in its mount on the ceiling. I think he was glad for the time to think as much as I was. When we finished, he turned to me and asked, "Can I hold you?"

The fact that he felt like he needed to ask brought tears to my eyes. "Of course," I said.

He wrapped me in his arms, the heat of his chest warming my cheek. He stroked my hair. "I'm sorry that I brought all this drama to our home."

"I think the drama-bringer left with your daughter." I'd tried to make it sound light, but my voice caught at the end. "We've postponed our wedding twice now, Doc. What if it's just not meant to happen? What if this is fate's way of telling us we can't work?"

His embrace tightened. "You are my mate, and there will be no more postponements. I don't care if I have to haul your cute ass to the justice of the peace, we'll be married by the end of the week."

"You have a highly developed sense of empathy, Doc. What if what you felt was pity when you cared for me for all those months, and you somehow convinced yourself it was something else?"

"I've never pitied you," he said, his tone low and serious. "You were tortured, bones broken and worse, your brother was laid to rest in front of you, and through it all, I saw you worry for your friend and for your brother, never for yourself."

"I did plenty of worrying for myself. I just didn't talk about it."

"You are the bravest woman I know, Chavvah. I am in love with you, and I mean to make it all nice a legal. Make no mistake. I would give up the world before I would give you up."

"What about Etta's mom? Robbie. Did you love her?"

He crooked a finger under my chin and tilted my head back so that I had to look up at him. I met his gaze. "I thought I did. But I left to pursue a career in medicine. I'd planned to finish my internship then come back to the tribe as a healer for them."

"Then your dad told you that she died."

He nodded. "Yes. And without her there, I had no good reason to go home, so I found another home."

"Peculiar," I said.

He nodded again. "Yes."

"But you would have gone back if she'd lived."

"Yes, I would have," he agreed. He kissed me gently. "But that's how I know."

"Know what?"

"That I didn't really love her. She was never mine, and I was never hers. Because if she had been you, I would have never left in the first place. Nothing would ever keep me from being with you. Nothing."

"She had your child."

"And didn't tell me she was pregnant. You don't do that to someone you really love."

"How do you feel?" I asked, fearful of the answer. "Knowing you have a daughter."

"Angry with my father. Sorry for Etta that she was raised by that man." He caressed my cheek. "Scared that I will lose you."

"I'm not naive, Doc. I know you had a life before me. After all, you're almost twice my age." I gave his hard abs a playful poke to take the edge off my words. "I can deal with a long, lost daughter. I just wish I knew why all this was happening. You know, now. I'm tired of getting my hopes up and having them kicked in their little lady balls. I want to marry you, probably more than I've wanted anything in my life. And I know that life has its mountains to climb, but I never thought I'd have to scale Everest." I sighed and sagged against him. "And what's with all the lycanthropes showing up all of a sudden?"

"I aim to find that information out tonight. I can't come up against my dad in the morning if I don't have all the facts."

"If you're going to the camp, I'm coming with you."

"It might be better if you stay here. A lycan cluster can be...hostile...to outsiders."

I leaned back and gave him a sharp look. "Are we in this together?"

The corner of his mouth quirked up in a lopsided smile. "We are."

"Then I'm coming with you."

He dipped his head and pressed his lips to mine. Tingles ran along my skin where his hands caressed and kneaded. He wove his fingers up the back of my neck and into my hair, giving my head a slight tug back as the kissed deepened into one that claimed and conquered. I moaned into his mouth as my body sizzled with burning need and desire, making me want to scale him like Everest.

I leaned my head back, gasping as he trailed hot kisses from my mouth to my neck.

"If you're trying... to distract... me.... from going... with you," I panted. "It's working."

His silver gaze met mine. "Where I go, you go. Where you are, I am. Always."

My own surge of claiming had me wrapping my legs around his waist as Billy Bob carried me to the kitchen counter and set me on the edge. I ripped his shirt off as he helped me out of my jeans before we both shoved his down around his thighs. And when he entered me swift, and with so much passion, I cried out with joy.

THE DOC and I had made love for over four hours, and when we'd finished, he'd barely given me enough time to run a brush through my hair, let alone shower, before we were out the door and on our way to the camp. The defecting lycans had taken up a small open space in a wooded area just outside the northern boundary of Peculiar, just on the edge our property. They'd set up about a dozen tents, a campfire at the center of the site, some coolers, two picnic tables, and a trash barrel thirty feet out from the living space. In a word, the campsite was neat and well-organized.

I don't know why, but it surprised me. Maybe because of my parents' prejudices when I was growing up. I'd been taught that werewolves were unpredictable savages. I knew better now. After all, I was part lycanthrope, and the love of my life was all wolfy-goodness, but it didn't stop me from having a preconceived notion that a were-wolf camp would look as if it were manned by frat boys with empty beer bottles strewn about, food half eaten and buzzing with flies, and trash all over the place.

It was close to midnight now, not terribly late, but the wayward tribe members were already in their tents. As we approached, two men and a woman came out of a large tent to greet us.

A man, a few inches shorter than Billy Bob, with sandy blond hair, light blue eyes, and a growth of beard smiled when he saw us. "Junior!" he said to Billy Bob. "I was wondering how long it would take you to come out and break bread."

"Dale Rivers," Billy Bob said. "What the hell are you doing here?"

"I got your call, Brother," he grinned. "Just like everyone here. We've been waiting on you for three days."

Sunny's violent visions had started three days earlier. It made sense now that they came with the lycanthropes. She'd always had an affinity for animals and shifters. I just wish I knew why these current episodes were taking such a physical toll on her body.

"You should have called," Billy Bob said. "We had no idea you all were out here."

The second man, slightly taller than Dale, with darker blond hair but the same light blue eyes, nodded. "Some of us still practice the old ways," he said. "You know, when your grandfather was still with us."

"And who are you?" Billy Bob asked.

"Why you remember my little brother, right? Cal was only ten the last time you were home, but the little fella followed us around all the time."

Doc smiled. "Not so little anymore."

"Nope," Cal agreed. He gave his brother a tolerant glance. "Not anymore."

"Anyhow," Dale said, "when thirty-six, at least that will admit to it, lycanthropes have the same dream telling us that our destiny is in Peculiar, we listened."

"Thirty-six?" I asked. "The way William talked, I thought he'd lost most of his people."

"He's lost everyone under the age of fifty," the woman said. She grinned at Billy Bob. "How's it going, Bobby Boy?"

"Joe," he countered. "I see you're still with this ugly cuss." He gestured to Dale.

Dale wrapped his arm around her shoulder. "We're going on thirty years now. I can't believe she hasn't killed me, yet."

The doc chuckled. "You and me both, Brother."

They shook hands then Dale grabbed Billy Bob in a bear

hug and picked him up off the ground. "It's damn good to see you. It really has been too long."

I stepped to the side of the reuniting friends. The woman whom Billy Bob had called Joe winked at me. "Those two were inseparable back in the day," she said. "Name's Joanna. You must be Chavvah the Spirit Talker."

"How in the world--"

"We heard your name on the wind about three years ago, maybe a little less." Joanna sniffed. "It was a kind of pain that called to us."

Billy Bob and I exchanged a look. It must have been during my captivity when Brother Wolf had first started speaking to me. "That's so weird," I said, as if I had no idea what she was talking about.

Then, when William got wind of your upcoming nuptials, and we heard your name it again, it seemed to make sense that our Bobby Boy went and found you." She laughed. "Besides, the fact that you've got Bobby's scent all over you seems to confirm that you're his girl."

Had the doc kept me from showering so I'd be covered in his smell? I glared up at Billy Bob, who did not meet my gaze, which pretty much confirmed my suspicions. I'd let it go since we were with company, but when we got back home, he was getting an earful.

"I thought William was going to have a stroke! We'd already lost most of the tribe under the age of thirty." She shook her head. "The last borns."

"How?"

"We haven't had a successful mating in over two decades. That doesn't hold much appeal for the young, so they left to integrate or find another home where they could be accepted." Joanna nodded at Billy Bob. "Much like him." She pursed her lips for a moment, then said, "Our own boy, Jake, is living in Tulsa, now. He works in construction there. I hope... Well, it doesn't matter. Whatever happens next happens. We'll trust in the spirits to guide us."

I wanted to tell her not to count on Brother Wolf, because he wasn't always reliable, but I could see how much she needed to believe. Frankly, I wanted to give her the hope she so badly needed. "You all should move your camp onto our property. Just in case the park rangers do any patrolling out here."

"Uhm," Doc said. "I don't--"

"Thank you, dear lady, for giving us refuge, comfort, and safety in your territory," Dale said quickly before Billy Bob could say more, then Dale nodded his head in reverence. "We accept your invitation."

Doc looked at me for a quick second like I'd sprouted horns and cloven feet, but he finally said to Dale, "Of course, you are all welcome."

CHAPTER FIVE

*D*ecember 20th. One day before the wedding..

Seven o'clock in the morning had come too soon, considering, we'd helped the thirty-six homeless lycanthropes relocate to the property. I was glad the weather had stayed clear and not too cold. If the lycans were anything like Billy Bob, they would run hot naturally, and wouldn't suffer much if the temperature dropped. We had an open field on the far side of the sweat lodge that was fairly flat, which made it a good site for a camp.

Unfortunately, William was due to arrive in two hours, and having all his people on our land would confirm his worst suspicions, that Billy Bob had indeed stole his tribe. All of this, the doc had explained to me at length until I'd shut him up with apology nookie that made us both feel better for a little while. But now, I was going on two hours of sleep, and I had no idea how we were going to sort any of this out. Neither Billy Bob nor I wanted the responsibility of leadership but inviting them in could be construed as accepting the position whether I'd meant it or not.

Argh! Stupid werewolf politics. Therianthropes had governing agencies all over the country, like the Tri-State Council, that created and enforced laws of behavior for our kind. But it was still more like a regular democracy. We could choose where we lived, how we lived, and who we lived with as long as it didn't break any of the rules. Apparently, the same couldn't be said about the lycan-thropes. Their lives were strictly regimented, and if they colored outside the lines, like moving away or marrying outside their species, then they were considered outcasts to be shunned.

Joanna had told me that she hadn't see her son Jake, who was now twenty-nine, for nearly ten years. Not since he'd chosen to leave the tribe behind to seek his own life. She had talked to him a couple of times from a pre-paid phone she'd bought from a gas station to keep William and his enforcers from finding out. I couldn't imagine what the forced separation must have been like for her. I mean, I'd spent years away from my mom and dad, but I always knew I could talk to and see them anytime I wanted.

"How come you were allowed to go off to school and return?" I asked Doc as he helped me prepare breakfast. "Was it because you were William's son?" I pulled the bacon apart as I waited for his answer.

"You can leave to pursue your education, you can even

take jobs out in the human world. Dale told me that his brother Cal was an officer for the Oklahoma Highway Patrol. As long as you live in the community, and you don't mix with outsiders when you're not at work, you are coloring within the lines of the tribal laws. I had planned to bring my skills back to White Rock, but with my grandfather gone and Robbie dead, I didn't see any reason to return. My father and I had been estranged since my childhood."

"After your mother died?" He'd never said much about her death, except that she'd passed quickly when he was nine-years-old.

Billy Bob shook his head. "He was always a hard man, even when my mom had been alive. When my grandfather invited me to learn the ways of the spirit, I'd jumped at the chance. It broke his heart when I'd joined the army, but still, I hadn't severed ties with our people, so I was allowed to return. My father blamed him for what he called my wandering soul. And they'd had a falling out when I was thirty, shortly before grandfather died, that made my dad turn away from our old ways. My dad wouldn't tell me what the fight had been about. Instead, he made the declaration that he was bringing the tribe into the modern century, and we would no longer follow the path of the spirit."

"Wow, that's the most you've ever told me about your past." I wrapped my arms around his waist, keeping my greasy fingers off his turquoise shirt. "I'm sorry about your grandfather."

"I'd planned to defy him. My dad, that is. I was going to continue my grandfather's work under the guise of providing only medical treatment."

"Like you do for the folks here in Peculiar." I craned my head back, and he kissed me for the effort.

"Yes, like I do here in Peculiar." He cupped my face. "My grandfather was more talented than me when it came to spirit talking. He could reach out with a few minutes of chants and reach Brother Wolf. It takes me hours to do the same. But you, my love, are a miracle. He comes to you when you need him without the need for ceremony."

"I don't know about all that. Brother Wolf has been ignoring me since the confrontation with your dad yesterday. I feel more like his puppet most of the time." I sighed. "I'm not being fair. I wouldn't have made it out of some the darker times in my life the past couple of years if it hadn't been for Brother Wolf. But, man, he can be so frustrating."

"And ambiguous," Billy Bob said. "Don't forget ambiguous."

"That's the worst. I mean, how hard is it to be specific." The sizzle of bacon in the pan redirected my attention. I let go of Billy Bob and grabbed the spatula. "Are you going to go check on our guests?"

"I supposed I should before my dad shows up."

"If I was really a miracle I'd cast an invisibility cloak over the bunch of them until William came and went. I'm not looking forward to his reaction. Why didn't you give me a heads up not to act neighborly with your buddies."

"It didn't occur to me that you would invite them to stay."

"As guests," I said in my defense. "But Dale turned it into something that I hadn't intended."

Billy Bob smiled, and I liked the way it lit his silver eyes. "Dale was always smart and quick. He's a lawyer. We haven't had one in town since..."

"Since Neville Lutjen was dealt with for his crimes against therians." And my own kidnapping, I didn't add, because the doc knew all too well what had been done to me so that Neville could keep his secrets.

"Yes, since then." He raised his brows at me. "They could be an asset to Peculiar."

"You know as well as I do that the town is going to take some convincing if you intend to add thirty-six wolves to the mix. They like you. Hell, they love you. But I'm not sure they'd love a whole herd of you moving in."

"Well, luckily, lycanthropes are just like anyone else. They are all unique with their own sets of skills, values, and personalities," he countered.

"And their own sets of problems." I flipped over the bacon and mashed the curling edges. "If you are seriously thinking about taking them under your protection, it is going to be an uphill climb."

"Under our protection," he said. He gave me a wry smile. "Remember, we're in this together."

THE KNOCK at the door around eight-thirty put a knot in my belly. Even with the new information, I felt ill prepared for a confrontation with William Smith. The knot loosened when I peeked out the window to see, not William, but Sunny holding Baby Jude who was now a rambunctious toddler, and a jumbo-sized diaper bag, Willy with her infant daughter, Willow, and another huge diaper bag, and Ruth, holding Sunny's other baby, Dawn, standing on my stoop.

I flung the door open. "What are you all doing here?"

Willy, in fiery red-head style, said, "If you think we're going to let anyone fuck with you on the day before your wedding, especially, a dick-headed in-law, you got another thing coming."

Both Ruth and Sunny, who had covered Jude's and Dawn's ears, nodded their agreement.

"Sunny called us last night," Ruth said. "And we made an executive decision to show up as your support team."

"Are the kiddos going to act as shields?"

Sunny gave me a sheepish grin. "Dakota is covering the breakfast shift this morning at Sunny's Outlook. She's going to come get them around ten-thirty." Dakota, Ruth's oldest daughter and a jack of all trades, had turned out to be a complete blessing during this crazy time, by taking over my shifts at the restaurant, but it had left Sunny without her normal babysitter."

Ruth blushed. "Michele would have taken them, but she had made a prior commitment."

Since her on-again boyfriend Jo Jo was working, and I knew Michele didn't have a regular job, I wondered at her prior commitment. Willy, who was Jo Jo's stepmom, gave a quick roll of her eyes, so I didn't ask.

"Well, come on in," I told them. "I'm happy for the support." Besides, I knew if William got too out of hand, all three of them were more than capable of showing him his place.

Billy Bob came out of the kitchen, an apron tied around his waist, and his hair pulled back to keep strays from falling in the food. He grimaced when he saw the BFF brigade.

"Ladies," he said.

Sunny whistled and said to me. "I do love a man in an apron."

"Does he do windows?" Willy asked. "Because he sure knows how to shine."

Ruth giggled. "It's hard not to love a man who will bring home the bacon *and* fry it up in a pan."

"Chavvah fried the bacon," he said deadpan. "Speaking of bacon. Does this mean we're having three more guests for breakfast?"

"This one can have my bacon." She gave Jude a poke in his belly and he laughed. "He can put away nearly as much as his father."

Sunny was a vegetarian, but not for the normal reasons. Her affinity for animals extended to the dead ones, and, as she explained it, when you experience your meal being slaughtered before your eyes, it curbs the appetite. But she'd given birth to coyote shifters, and coyotes were carnivores.

She set Jude down and he ran as fast as his little feet could take him right over to Billy Bob. "Uncle!" he said excitedly. "Rocket!"

The ceiling in the living room was vaulted and Billy Bob picked up the boy and threw him several feet in the air before catching him and swinging him around. Jude squealed with delight.

The doc beamed with joy. He'd taken on the roll as uncle to Babe and Sunny's children with relish. Again, I couldn't help but feel like I was depriving him of his own family. He caught my look and set Jude down.

He took the boy's hand. "Want to help me in the kitchen?"

Jude answered by bouncing on his toes and following Billy Bob out of the room.

When we were alone, Willy blatantly asked, "So what's this I hear about the doc having a kid, and who the fuck are all those people in your pasture?"

CHAPTER SIX

*T*he conversation about Etta and our new lodgers was short, because no sooner did I give a brief breakdown to get my girls up to speed, William and Etta arrived.

"Why are my people on your land?" William growled as he pushed his way inside the house. He spoke to Billy Bob, not me, treating me as inconsequential. "I guess you've made your choice, son."

"I didn't make any decision," Billy Bob said as he walked out of the kitchen with Jude on his hip. "Your people walked away from you. The decision was theirs."

"But it was your decision to accept them and take them under your protection." He stopped a few feet short of the doc, and I could see the relief on Sunny's face as I retrieved Jude from his favorite uncle.

"No rough stuff in front of the kiddos," I said.

Willow, only a few months old, flipped in her mom's arms, and turned into a werecougar. She let out an irritated hiss, and I nodded. Even a tiny baby could sense the tension in this room.

That's when I noticed Etta expression. It wasn't hard and angry like the night before. She was staring at Jude, Dawn, and Willow, her eyes wide with something akin to awe.

"Do you want to hold him?" I asked her.

"How old is he?" she said.

"He'll be three in February." I walked closer to Etta, holding tight to my squirmy nephew. "Here. He won't bite."

Sunny chuckled. "That's a lie."

"Don't mind Sunny. Jude is a friendly little cuss," Ruth said.

Etta reluctantly held out her hands, and I handed Jude off.

"Oh my gosh," she said. "He's so light."

"Therianthrope babies mature more slowly than human children, but they catch up by the time they are in their late teens," Sunny said. "Or so I've been told. Is it different for lycanthropes?"

Etta shrugged. "I don't know."

"I'm sorry," Sunny said.

"So, is he my brother?" Etta asked.

"No," I told her with a gentle smile. "He's my brother and Sunny's son, so in a way that makes him your cousin."

"Oh." She didn't try to hide her disappointment.

"Is this the first time you've held a child?" I asked.

Etta nodded. "I'm the youngest in our town." Jude pulled on her hair and said loudly, "Like Uncle!"

"Yes," I told him. "Like Uncle's hair."

The girl carefully put Jude down, her face unreadable. "Father, we should go."

"Not until I get my people back," William said. He'd been quiet through the entire exchange between us, but it had only been a short pause in his agenda. "I claim the right of *lupiduci*."

"Don't be ridiculous, Father," Billy Bob said.

William's face flamed with color. "Ridiculous is letting you, a *proditor*," he spat the word. "A traitor, take what's mine."

Billy Bob's back straightened as he leaned in toward his father and said with more menace than I'd ever heard from him, "Like you took what's mine when you deprived me of my child?"

"Stop it," Etta said. "I am not your child. You gave up any rights to me when you left our tribe."

"Is that what he told you?" Billy Bob asked. "I would have come back for you if I had known you existed."

Etta hesitated then shook her head. "Father warned me not to trust you."

The veins over Billy Bob's muscles popped out visibly as I watched him work to hold his temper in check. "He is a liar. The fact that you don't know that about him tells me you are either blind, or he has gotten better at acting over the years."

The smoke alarm went off in the kitchen again. "We got it," Sunny said, corralling Ruth, Willy, and the kids.

Willy stopped to give William a fierce stare, well, as fierce as a tiny woman could while carrying a cute little kitten in her arms. "We'll just be around the corner if you need us," she told me, and with that, they all went into the kitchen.

I heard broomstick whack the fire alarm again. I'd have to buy a new one if this became a trend.

"Fixed!" Sunny shouted triumphantly. "And only a couple of pieces of bacon are burnt! Breakfast salvaged."

"Are we going to eat or fight?" I asked the warring wolves.

"Pick your second," William said.

"I'm not choosing someone to fight my battles. I will take on your champion myself."

The barest hint of smile tugged at William's lips for a microsecond then it disappeared. "I choose Etta. She is my best warrior."

Billy Bob looked as if he'd been struck. "No."

Etta looked just as surprised.

"You can't want this, Father," Billy Bob said.

"Etta is proficient in all forms of combat, including swords. I have faith in her victory." He narrowed his gaze on the doc. "What I wanted was my people back, but I will take your defeat as a consolation prize."

Billy Bob looked at his adult daughter and shook his head. "This isn't right. I refuse your challenge."

"*Lupiduci* dictates the ritual. You can dictate the terms." William lifted his hands in an amiable gesture. "It doesn't have to be to the death. First person to draw blood wins."

"No," he said. "I won't pick up a sword against her."

William's face lit up with triumph. He knew Billy Bob would refuse to fight Etta, and he wasn't above using his own flesh and blood to get his way. "Then you lose, and by the rite of *lupiduci*, you must turn the tribe away."

"You know that won't stop them from leaving you," Billy Bob said.

"No, but it will make them lone wolves by all tribal standards. Outcasts. Like you, son. They will no longer have any standing in any lycanthropic community."

The more William blathered, the more rage I felt for Billy Bob, the lycans out in our field, and even Etta. The elder Smith really was a master manipulator. He was still summarizing all that Billy Bob and the wayward members would be giving up, when Brother Wolf told me, *this must not stand, little sister*.

I know, I thought back to him. *But what can I do?*

You know.

I don't, I told him. *I need you to tell me.* But Brother Wolf was silent once again.

The bickering between father and son was escalating.

You know. Thanks for the vague directions, Brother Wolf. I absolutely did not know the right thing to do, but impulsively, I said, "I'll do it. I'll be Doc's second."

I heard plates clattering in the kitchen as they hit the floor, and my three besties hustled out to the living room.

"No, no, no," Sunny said. "You are getting married tomorrow, Chav. Brides-to-be don't pick sword fights."

"I won't let you fight my battle," Billy Bob said. "It's not your place."

"My place is by your side. We're in this together. Remember? You are my first, so let me be your second." I eyeballed Etta who stood at least an inch taller than me, and she had well-defined muscles in her arms. "Besides, it's not to the death, right?"

Etta snorted. "You think you can take me? I have bested all challengers since I was nineteen. You really don't want to mess with me, lady."

"We'll see about that," I said. "How long do I have to prepare?"

"We will fight on the solstice," Etta said, "as ritual dictates. Lucky us, we won't have to wait long. The next one is tomorrow."

Sunny gasped. "That's your wedding night! I'll say it again, no, no, no."

"It won't take long," Etta said, her voice brimming with confidence. "Once I make quick work of you, you'll have plenty of time to marry this traitor. As a bonus, I won't even mark your face. You'll still be pretty for your pictures."

"Aww," Sunny said. "Your new stepdaughter thinks you're pretty."

I couldn't think of an appropriate comeback, so I crossed my arms over my chest and gave her a *come-at-me* look.

William cast his granddaughter a quick look and said, "Let's go, Etta. We must prepare for tomorrow."

After they left, Billy Bob stormed off to the clinic side of our place. I looked at my three girls, all of their expressions grim and worried. "What?" I asked. "I had to do something. I've met those people, and besides..." Could I really blame Brother Wolf? After all, he hadn't specifically told me to get into a fight with my new in-laws. "We have lots of food. Who's hungry?"

"These days, I'm always hungry," Willy said. Her eyes widened as we all turned our gazes on her. "Oh, shit. I was going to wait until after the wedding to tell you all." She put her hand on her belly. "Preggers again."

I joined the chorus of congratulations, wishing I could feel as happy for her as I sounded. I'd become a pretty good actor as well.

When I hugged Willy, she whispered in my ear, "Don't worry. This little alien inside me won't stop me from teaching you some tricks that will turn you into an ass-kicker in no time. Just don't tell Brady. He's such a hoverer."

"It'll be our secret." I added a grateful, "thank you," because I was currently as far away as a person could get from being an ass-kicker, and I needed all the help I could get.

Then Sunny said, "Chav, I think we should pack a bag and get you out of town. Maybe you and the doc should just elope."

"I'm doing this." The words came out more forcefully than I'd intended.

"You remember I had a vision of Etta with blood all over her hands." She twirled her hand around for emphasis. "Like lots of it. What if I was seeing your blood?"

Ruth worried her lower lip between her teeth. "Eloping is good. Ed and I could use a vacation, and since our Reno trip was such a dud, I wouldn't mind trying Vegas."

"Same," said Willy. "Brady and I could use a little honeymoon time before the next baby comes."

Everything they were saying sounded really tempting, but I couldn't. I barely knew the lycans who had arrived, but a part of me knew that I had to try whatever I could to protect them.

"I appreciate the escape plan," I told my three worried pals, "but this is a story that will have to play out, regardless of the outcome." I couldn't lie to myself, though. Sunny's vision had me concerned. Why was all this happening now? My fantasy wedding was quickly turning into a nightmare.

Ten minutes after William and Etta had made their dramatic exit, there was another knock at the front door. Considering Doc still hadn't come back from the clinic, and I'd spent those long minutes getting lectured by Sunny, Ruth, and Willy, I was glad for the reprieve.

Dale, Joanna, and Cal Rivers stood just outside, their faces mirroring my own concern.

"We saw William leave," Dale said. "We've come to ask if you are revoking your invitation."

"No," I said. "Why don't you come in for some breakfast. I've got enough food to feed an army in here, and no army."

Joanna smiled. "We can definitely supply the hungry soldiers." She glanced over her shoulder toward the field of tents then cast me an apologetic smile. "We ran out of provisions yesterday."

"I'm not sure I have enough for all thirty-six of you..." Damn it, I felt the fool. I'd invited all these people onto the property without thinking what it would mean to anyone. I'd only meant to be polite, but I'd really stuck my foot in it.

"I'll call Sunny's Outlook and we can have trays of eggs, toast, and hash browns, and cinnamon rolls on their way in an hour," Sunny said. "The breakfast rush should be over by then."

Ruth chimed in next. "I bet Blondina could whip us up a stack of ham steaks, and we can buy out all the donuts from Becky's Bakery. Dakota can pick them up on the way over here."

Blondina Messer owned The Blonde Bear Cafe in town with her husband Roger. They served the best burgers in town. Becky Baker, an eagle shifter, made the best confections, including the delicious lemon cream wedding cake with a raspberry center she was making for our nuptials on Friday. "I bet they'd even give us a bulk discount," I said.

Willy nodded. "I'll call Brady. He and Jo Jo can haul the food from Sunny's Outlook and Blonde Bear Cafe over here."

I looked at Dale and Joanna. "If you all can wait about an hour, an hour and a half, we can have breakfast set up for everyone, buffet style."

The wolf shifter grinned. "Darling, you sure no how to get things done."

I glanced at my friends. "With a lot of help."

"We'll let the others know," Joanna said. "And when we're all together, you can tell us what happened with William and Etta."

"Deal," I said. Baby Jude smacked at my leg, and I picked him up.

"Auntie Chav." He pressed his wet mouth to my cheek. "Kisses."

Joanna laughed as tears crested her eyes. "Also, promise we get to hold the babies."

"As long as it's okay with the babies and the babies' moms," I said, forcing a smile. I could have all the baby time I wanted with my nephew and nieces, and I was still heartbroken I couldn't have my own child. I couldn't imagine what the past twenty-one years must have been like for these folks. Jude blew a raspberry against my neck and giggled. I laughed. "They really do love the attention."

"They are total hams," Sunny agreed.

After a short goodbye, the Rivers left to inform the group about breakfast. I looked at my own army of soldiers. The ramifications of the past two days started to settle in on me. I fought back the tears threatening to spill if I gave them a chance.

"I'm so screwed."

Sunny choked on a nervous laugh, and said, "Oh, honey. You really are."

CHAPTER SEVEN

$\mathcal{T}$he BFF brigade organized the food while I headed into the clinic to try and make amends with my guy. The clinic was closed this week to non-emergent patients, so Billy Bob busied himself with paperwork in his office. Therianthropes in Missouri, Arkansas, and Kansas had medical insurance through the Tri-State Council's care plan. Billy Bob made it a practice of billing the council, then writing off whatever they didn't cover, which meant, the people in Peculiar had full universal coverage, with the few exceptions of tests and treatments he couldn't perform in his office, like CAT scans, MRIs, radiation for cancer, and such. Thankfully, therians rarely suffered from major illnesses and diseases. It was a gift of our genetics to be hardy and long-lived.

I tapped on his open door. "Hey, Doc."

"Hey," he said as he signed the bottom of a claim form.

I sagged my hip against the doorframe. "You mad at me?"

"I'm not happy." He put his pen down, his silver gaze shifting in my direction. "How could you volunteer to fight Etta?"

"It's not to the death," I said in my defense.

"Thank heavens," he said, "because, I know the training my father has put her through. Etta will be highly skilled at fighting. The last time I checked, you were highly skilled at cooking, not combat." He growled under his breath. "These fights can get nasty, Chav. Emotions run high. What if Etta goes for more than just first blood?"

Exasperation, resentment, and a lot of irritation colored what I said next. "I had to do something. You might not feel responsible for those people out there, but I do. We invited them--"

"You invited them," he corrected.

"Fine." I threw up my hands. "I invited them in. And while I didn't know what I was getting myself into, I would do it again. Those are your people, Billy Bob."

They are your people, too, little sister, Brother Wolf whispered.

"Oh, shut up."

Billy Bob narrowed his eyes at me.

"Not you." I pointed to my head. "Brother Wolf."

"Is he talking to you now? Ask him why he has brought all this trouble to our door."

Brother Wolf was radio silent.

I crossed my arms over my chest and narrowed my gaze back at the doc. "He's not saying. But that's not the point."

"Then what's the point?"

"The point is, regardless of why or how the lycanthropes ended up on our doorstep, I am not going to let your dad mess us or them about. He only chose Etta as his second to get you to back down. He is using her to take the fight out of you, and it feels like he's been waiting her whole life for this moment."

Billy Bob looked down for a moment, then back to me, his expression sad and tired. "I can't lose you. If anything happens to you, I will hate my own daughter. I don't want to hate her, Chav."

"I can't let William win," I said. I crossed the room to his desk, and he scooted his chair back to make room for me on his lap. "We can't let him win. I may not be from your tribe, but I am your mate, and these people, well, they can have a good life here in Peculiar."

"You know lycans play by different rules than therians, right?"

"You learned a different way," I said. "So, can they."

"If you win."

"I will win." Or at least I'd try really hard. I gave Billy Bob a quick kiss. "Now, stop your brooding. We have guests coming in about an hour for breakfast."

Billy Bob frowned. "Are William and Etta coming back?"

"No, this will be just a few of our closest friends and thirty-six lycanthropes." I made myself smile and worried it hadn't reach my eyes. "Sunny and the gang are arranging the food. I think the lycans are running low on supplies."

He slid his hand down my back to give my butt a friendly squeeze. "You're a good woman, Chavvah Trimmel."

I turned in his lap until I was straddling his thighs. I rubbed myself against him. "And you're a hard man, Billy Bob Smith." I leaned forward and nipped his ear. "Just the way I like you."

"We have an hour," he said, nuzzling my neck. "I can work with that."

I laughed as he picked me up and carried me into one of the empty recovery rooms, and we set about destroying the hospital corners on the small twin bed.

SUNNY AND OUR Scooby gang had the food situation under control, so I used the opportunity to jump in the shower. Therians and lycans might not be all that modest about their bodies, but I'd grown up an integrator, living amongst humans, and I still had a few hang ups about privacy. I made quick work of towel drying my hair and putting in a single braid down the back so that I wouldn't have to worry about breaking out the blow dryer. By the time I dressed, the werewolves, along with Brady, Jo Jo, Babe, Sheriff Sid Taylor, Blondina and Roger Messer, my mom, Dakota, and Luke Dwyer, a deer shifter Dakota was currently dating, along with the thirty-six lycans had all arrived. Luckily, it was warming up to be close to fifty degrees in the late morning sun, so most everyone had stayed outside instead of trying to crowd into the house.

Billy Bob was directing the wolves to set up eight tables outside that Blondina and Roger had been prescient enough to bring with enough seating for fifty-four people, and still have an extra table for the food, so that folks could fix their own plates. Brady had been smart enough to grab the sixty-cup coffee maker from the community center, along with six gallons of milk and six gallons of orange juice, along with several bags of Styrofoam cups. The way they'd all come together to feed a bunch of strangers made me swell with pride. I might not know everyone in Peculiar, but when it came down to it, this town was a large family, and we took care of our own. As I watched the lycanthropes work alongside the therians, I hoped that someday soon they would know what it was like to feel this supported all the time.

"Hey, Sis," Babe said, as he brushed his shoulder against mine. "You want to tell me what the hell you've gotten yourself into with all this?"

"It's wonderful," I said. "Isn't it."

He raised a brow at me. "You're a little crazy, aren't you?"

I shrugged. "Speaking of crazy, who invited mom to this shindig?"

"She was at the courthouse with me when Sunny called. I couldn't just leave her there."

I nodded to the sheriff. "And Sid?"

"Yep, he was there as well. Since we don't have a judge, he's been presiding over some of the smaller cases that don't need to be kicked up to the Tri-State Council."

"Well, I suppose he would've found out eventually." Considering we'd asked him to perform our wedding ceremony, and I didn't think I'd be able to keep the fight from any of the guests, let alone our officiator.

"How long do you think they'll be here?"

"If I have my way?" I looked him directly in the eye. "For as long as they want."

"Now, Sis..."

I waved at Joanna, who was currently swinging Jude up in the air. "I better go mingle with my guests," I told him and walked away. I wasn't ready to have this conversation with Babe, yet, and the fact that he wasn't yelling at me, told me that Sunny hadn't given him the complete rundown of the situation.

"Foods on," Willy hollered. "There's plenty, so eat up."

Billy Bob, who'd been chatting with several of the lycan

men, came up to me and put his arms around me. "In case I haven't told you, you're pretty amazing."

"You have," I said. "But a girl never tires of hearing it."

Dale joined us. "I overheard your friends talking. The blonde woman and the red-head with the mouth. Is it true? Is Chav going to fight Etta in the *lupiduci* rite? You've named her as your second."

I groaned. It wouldn't be long until Babe, my mom, and everyone else knew. So much for a brief pause in the drama.

"That would be Sunny and Willy," Billy Bob said. "And I didn't name her." His expression soured. "She named herself."

"She is right here," I said. "And, yes, I volunteered."

"You must be a great warrior," Dale said.

Billy Bob tightened his hold on me. "She is a survivor."

Sure, we could go with that. I'd survived hunters who'd tortured me and planned to kill me, and I'd survived being kidnapped twice by serial killing twins who had wanted to skin me alive. "I don't plan to lose," I said. It didn't mean I wouldn't, but I didn't have to tell Dale that.

"The tribe stands with you," Dale said. He bowed his head slightly. "We will lend you our strength when the time comes."

"Thanks," I said. "I'll take it."

Billy Bob gave me another, *what are you doing?* look. What the heck had I gotten wrong this time?"

I gave him an, *I don't know what I'm doing. Like at all. Haven't you figured that out by now?* look.

"It's so nice to be around children again," Dale said, adeptly changing the subject. "It's been too long."

I cast him a grateful glance. "This town isn't lacking in the baby department, that's for sure."

He smiled. "I'm sure you two can't wait to get started on your own family."

I wasn't prepared to explain my circumstances, so instead, I nodded.

He continued, "When Jake was born, Joanna and I thought we'd have time for more." His gaze trailed over to Willow, who was being passed around and cuddled by several of the lycan women. "A daughter would have made her happy." He shook his head. "We were lucky, though. We're the only ones here who had a child before the tribe became infertile."

"Were any of you tested? I mean, by a doctor."

Dale nodded. "Over the years, several couples, including Joanna and I, went to specialists to try and figure out what was wrong. According to the experts, all our parts are working parts. The swimmers are swimming, the eggs are dropping. Pierce and Debbie Jones" he pointed to a couple who were playing with Dawn, "even went as far as doing that invitro fertilization, but all the embryos failed to take. William has taken our town so far from the old traditions, many of us feel like this is our punishment for letting him."

I'd never thought of Brother Wolf as vengeful, but over two decades without any pregnancies, seemed to imply he was just that.

I don't require worship, if that is what you're implying, little sister.

I was simply musing, Brother Wolf. I wasn't implying anything.

I could feel his sharp disapproval. *Lycanthropes are not like therianthropes in origin. They are my creation, and I am flawed. Therefore, they are flawed.*

"So, how do I fix this?" I asked.

Both Dale and Billy Bob looked at me.

Dale said, "If I knew, I wouldn't keep it to myself."

"I'm sorry." I'd been frustrated enough with Brother Wolf to ask the question out loud.

Billy Bob put his hand on his old friend's shoulder. "Why don't you go get some food? We can talk about all this later."

"Back off!" someone shouted. I looked up to see Luke Dwyer facing off with Cal Rivers. Crap on a cracker, this was all I needed. Dakota's face was red and angry. Jo Jo was standing behind Luke, and a few of the younger lycans were gathering behind Cal. I groaned. If the wolves were going to integrate with the town, we were getting off to a bad start.

I ran up to them and placed myself between the two glowering men, Billy Bob on my heels. "What in the world is going on?"

I cast an accusing glance at Cal and was sharply put in my place when Dakota said, "Luke is completely overreacting. I'd tripped over a rock, and all this guy did was keep me from landing on my face."

"Don't be stupid, D. He has been eyeballing you since we got here. He probably tripped you himself."

Ruth, who'd also jumped into the mix, snapped her fingers at Luke. "Lucas Dwyer, I'll thank you not to call my daughter stupid. Now. Go. Home."

Cal, whose veins were popping from his forehead, leaned in. "Yeah, Lucas. Go. Home."

I snapped my fingers at Cal. "There's no call to make things worse."

He calmed down enough to look a little contrite. "Sorry, ma'am. I don't know what came over me." He glanced in Dakota's direction as Ruth escorted her into the house and then away, letting me know exactly what had come over him.

"It doesn't matter now," Billy Bob said. "It's over."

Babel came up after the kerfuffle. "If you guys are planning to move a bunch of lycanthropes into town, I think you are going to have more incidents like the one that almost happened here. We should call a town council meeting and talk about it. Sid and I both have concerns."

"How about if we wait until after the wedding?" I looked around. There was a tension in everyone that hadn't been there moments before. However, if I couldn't win this loopy doopy ritual on the solstice, whether the werewolves were allowed into the town or not would be a moot point. "You can make it my wedding gift," I told him.

"What are you guys talking about?" Sunny asked.

"The wedding," Babe said, looking none too happy with me.

"Oh, good," Sunny said with a sigh of relief. "Chav told you about having to fight Xena, Princess Werewolf."

"What?" His brow furrowed at me. "Fighting who? What? I think you better tell me everything."

I glared at Sunny. "Thanks for that."

"Whoops," she said. "I guess the wolf's out of the bag now. I'll be over at the donuts if anyone needs me."

CHAPTER EIGHT

*A*t the beginning of this week, all I'd wanted was to wear a beautiful dress as I exchanged vows with my hot husband to be in front of a few hundred of our family and friends. My biggest problems had been what flavor of cake to choose, and whether to go with red roses and white carnations or something more seasonal for the bouquet. Now, I would have to perform the lycanthrope version of the gladiator games as a prequel to the "I dos" in order to satisfy a ritual claim against Billy Bob, and on top of that I had Babel and Mom breathing down my neck about it. After the meal concluded and everyone had gone their own way, the townies back to town and the lycanthropes back to their tents, my mom and brother cornered me in the back of the house in a guest room.

"I knew getting involved with his kind was a bad idea," Mom said. "Someone like your Billy Bob might be able to work against his nature, but you put together a group of them, and you are just asking for trouble. Look at what happened earlier with that boy."

"The boy started it, according to Dakota Thompson," I said.

Mom ignored me. "And now, they expect you to fight one of them? It's too much, Chavvah Adine Trimmel. I won't have it. You need to call this off now."

"The fight or the wedding?" I asked.

"Both!" she said, her eyes bugging a little.

"Now, Mom," Babe said. "You were just saying how happy you were for Chav, not more than a couple of hours ago."

"That was before I realized she was playing out the live action version of *Game of Thrones* in her own front yard!"

"I'm a grown adult with the ability to make my own decisions," I told her. "At the last time I checked, I don't need your permission to marry or fight whoever I want."

"I've already lost one of my children," she said, referencing our older brother Judah. "I won't lose you, too."

"If you don't stop trying to control me, you're going to lose me anyhow."

"I'd prefer you alive and hating me than dead." Her words cut like ice through my veins.

I raised my emotional walls and slammed the doors shut between us. "Careful what you wish for." I pushed past her, but Babe grabbed my arm to stop me. "Let go of me," I told him.

He let go. "Why are your eyes golden?"

Crap. My wolf had pushed through to the surface. I could feel its frustration. It mirrored my own. "You know what I am," I told him. "I'm different from you and mom. I have a different destiny."

I rushed from the room toward the back door, shedding my clothes before my hand touched the knob. As soon as I was outside, I transformed into my timber wolf form, the white and brown fur spreading over my skin as I went from two feet to four paws.

"Hey!"

I turned my head over my shoulder to see Billy Bob standing in the doorway. I whined, hoping he would understand that I needed a few minutes alone. He nodded his head, stepped back, and closed the door between us.

I KNEW the property well enough to avoid the briars and stickems. Even in December, those thorny plants could be problematic for thick fur. Even so, it didn't take me long to find my way down to the creek where I'd tried to hide when Brother Wolf first made himself known to me. I swam across to the other side and leapt up onto a large rock and laid down to dry and think. I'd been acting on pure instinct of late, and I was beginning to wonder if my actual brain still worked. Mom and Babe weren't wrong to worry for me. Hell, I was worried for me. My impulsivity had landed me in a fight on what was supposed to be a happy day. The day I would finally become Mrs. Billy Bob Smith.

Was I somehow sabotaging myself? I'd already postponed twice now. The first time I'd called it off because I'd been afraid I'd never be the woman the doc needed. He'd convinced me otherwise and at great lengths. Luckily, we'd only set a date at that point, and so we just switched it to late summer. I'm not a hundred percent sure why I changed it the second time. I'd gotten a strong feeling that we needed to wait until the winter solstice. Again, Billy Bob supported me. I couldn't cancel again. I wouldn't. And, unlike the first two times, I had no intention of waffling one more. This was the exact right moment. I knew it in my bones.

I waited for a moment, half expecting Brother Wolf to chime in with some platitude.

Nothing. For a spirit guide, he was distinctly lacking in the guidance department.

I heard a rustling in the dried fallen leaves. Alert, I stood up and pointed my nose in the direction of the sound. It was a wolf, that much I knew. I waited as the racket grew louder, tense as the unexpected guest grew closer.

A silver wolf came out from behind a large oak.

Damn it, Billy Bob. I knew he was worried, but after my

confrontation with my mom, I'd just needed a minute to myself.

I cast a sideways glance at the wolf, startled at its size. This silver wolf was smaller than my mate, on top of that, its nose was slimmer and its tail shorter. Which meant, this wasn't him. I shook water from my fur as my hackles lifted on the back of my neck. I bared my teeth and growled.

The silver wolf appeared unconcerned. When it transformed into its bipedal form, Etta was kneeling in front of me. She stood up to her full height then, and said, "We should talk."

I changed into my human self, sat down, and wrapped my arms around my knees. "I think there will be enough talking tomorrow night."

"There you are wrong," she said. She pressed her fists against either side of her hips. "There will be a short amount of fighting and a lot of crying, but very little talking."

In a way, I admired her confidence. She was still so young. I'd had a lot of bravado when I was her age. I'd been ready to take on the world.

Unfortunately, Etta had a much narrower goal. She only wanted to take on me. "So, can we talk now?" she asked.

"Sure," I said. "Why not? You go first."

"Is it true?"

"Is what true?"

"That William, I mean, Billy Bob, didn't know about me until yesterday."

"True," I confirmed. "He had no idea."

"It doesn't matter," she said, but I could tell it did. "He always had one foot in and one foot out of our tribe. I could never have competed with his wanderlust."

"Is that what you think? That he would have chosen the world over you?" I picked at a piece of loose rock near my big toes. "Then I am really sad for you, because you don't have any idea what kind of man your father is."

"No," she said. "I don't. He wasn't around to give me any other idea." She crossed her arms. "And, he's not my father. William is. He raised me."

"You mean he brainwashed you," I said.

Etta's gaze narrowed on me as her cheeks pinked in anger. "He has given me shelter, food, and safety," she said, "and all he asked for in return is loyalty. I can give him that."

I gentled my tone. "I noticed you left out love."

Etta hesitated for a moment, then said, "He loves me."

"That's why he used you to manipulate Billy Bob, right? Because that's what loving parents do." I shook my head. "There's a reason he lost his son, and it's not because Billy Bob is incapable of loving. He is the most steadfast, caring man I've ever met."

Etta snorted, her annoyance clear. "You mean weak. He has forced his mate to fight me."

"He didn't force me. I volunteered," I amended. "And he refused to fight because you are his child. He doesn't want to publicly shame you or worse hurt you."

"He knows I would win."

"Keep telling yourself that."

"I will beat you when we fight," she said matter-of-factly.

"Maybe." I hopped down from the rock. "Probably. But I will have to have faith that the right outcome will prevail."

"And what do you think that is?"

"That I will be able to save Billy Bob's people. That I will be able to give them a chance at a life here with us." I gave her a pointed look. "That includes *all* his people."

Etta stared at me for a few moments as if trying to figure out what angle I was playing, then she said, "If you are trying to get me to throw the fight, I won't do it. I am acting second to William, our leader, and I won't bring shame on our family name."

"Of course not," I said. "William has already brought enough shame to the Smith name with his actions."

Etta didn't deny the accusations. "Be ready, Chavvah Trimmel. The solstice will come soon."

I nodded to her. "I'll be ready."

With a flourish, she was back in wolf form and trotting off into the woods.

Well done, little sister, Brother Wolf said when I was alone.

"I don't know about that," I said. "It feels a little bit like poking the bear, and I certainly didn't change Etta's mind about kicking my ass."

But you changed her heart a little, and that is progress.

"Well, if you can show me how to use progress as a shield against a sword, I'd greatly appreciate it."

Keep your sense of humor, my child. You will need it.

"Thank you, Brother Wolf. Helpful as always."

CHAPTER NINE

*M*uch to my relief, Billy Bob had kicked my mom and Babe out of the house while I'd been gone. I showered again, washing the creek from my body, and when I came out of the bedroom, Billy Bob was sitting on our bed.

"Did you get all your thinking done?" he asked.

"Yes," I said as I wrapped my hair in the towel. "No. Not really. If anything, I'm more confused than ever. Do you think there is some bigger plan here? Maybe Brother Wolf is planning to take over my body during the fight and eat Etta."

Billy Bob's looked aghast. "Don't even joke about that."

He'd been present while I was in Brother Wolf's avatar and I'd swallowed a whole serial killer in one gulp. "Who says I'm joking? She's one tough cookie. I'm going to need all the tricks in my arsenal."

"Please don't eat my daughter," he said.

"I'll make the request to Brother Wolf. Although, you could always go out to your sweat lodge and make the request yourself. Hell, you might even get more answers from him than he gives me. After all, I may have more direct access, but only when he wants me to."

"I may try. I'm as confounded as you are by what's going on."

"You're not going to try and talk me out of fighting, are you? I need your support right now, not your doubts."

"I love your independence and your stubborn streak, Chav. I never doubt you, and I trust that you make the choices best for you and the people you love. Besides, I know there's no talking you out of anything. I was foolish to even try."

I kissed him for the admission. "It takes a strong man to trust the way you do. Also, just so I don't feel like I'm keeping stuff from you, Etta was out in the woods earlier in wolf form."

Billy Bob stood up. "Why? Did she try to fight you?"

"No. Nothing like that. She just wanted to talk. I think she was surprised to find out that you didn't know about her. She wondered if you were lying." I caressed his cheek. "I told her that you would not have left her behind if you had known she existed."

"What else?" he asked.

"Well, she let me know in no uncertain terms that she planned to kick my ass. She's loyal, like you. Even if she's misguided." I half-smiled. "I think under different circumstances, I could really like her. I think she realizes that William is using her, but she feels like she owes him, which puts her firmly on his side.

"Well, I am on your side, sweetheart. Always. And speaking of on your side, Sunny and Willy are back, and Willy says to put on your stretchy clothes, because she's about to school you in sword fighting one-oh-one."

I bit back a groan. "Oh, yeah. I forgot about that. I'd rather crawl in bed with you." It was three o'clock in the afternoon, so there were still a few hours until dark. "But I suppose I should at least put in some effort to learn the basics."

"I agree on both counts," he said then kissed me again. "Get dressed. I'll let them know you're on your way."

"THIS IS NOT how we planned your bachelorette party," Sunny complained. "There was going to be drinking and strippers and pin the penis on the man."

Willy shook her head as we walked out to a clearing beyond tent city. "There wasn't going to be drinking or strippers," she said, swinging around a small sword with a leather wrapped hilt and a polished steel blade.

"But we were going to play pin the penis on the man?" I

held an identical sword in my own hand, marveling at how well-balanced it felt.

"It was Sunny's plan," Willy said. "Sort of like pin the tail on the donkey, only naughtier."

Sunny giggled. "I saw it on Pinterest. It looked like fun."

I gave the sword a little swing. "Where in the world did you get these, Willy?"

"I have a stash," she said. She wiggled her brows. "Don't tell Brady. I've had to hide my trunk of weapons since Willow was born, especially after Brady threatened to throw it in the lake."

"She keeps them at the sheriff's station," Sunny said. "Brady knows."

Willy flipped Sunny off.

Sunny stuck out her tongue. "Well, let's get this party started," she said. "Try not to cut off anything important."

I looked at Willy, who was going through several skilled moves moving in a backward and forward dance. "Just for clarification," I said. "Everything's important."

She stopped, leaned forward with a slight bow and tapped the flat of the blade to her forehead. "You ready?"

"No," I said honestly. "But let's do it."

One hour in to the training, and I could say with the utmost confidence, "I really suck at this." I'd stumbled like a klutz, swung the sword like a softball bat or a club, even though Willy had constantly reminded me not to leave my torso wide open. And while she never cut me once, I'd almost impaled myself when I rushed her, over balanced forward, and tumbled head over heels. "I've got zero chance."

"It's not that bad," Willy said.

"Yes, it is," my savagely honest bestie quipped. "You really are terrible at this."

"We will spend all night at if that's what it takes," Willy said.

By this time, the lycanthropes had begun to gather around us in a big circle. Dale and Joanna joined hands and all the other members joined suit until the circle was a closed loop.

Billy Bob came from the direction of the sweat lodge. He ducked between two of the werewolves. "There hasn't been a power pull since my grandfather was young man," he said.

Dale nodded. "If Chavvah truly is our new leader, we will be able to lend her our strength."

"Wait a minute. I thought that was just a statement of support earlier. You mean, you actually think you can transfer your strength to me? And what do you mean leader? I can barely lead my way out of paper bag?"

"Every tribe needs a leader and a shaman. Billy Bob is a shaman. You are our leader. We saw it in our dreams,"

Joanna said. "We saw a promise for a future we thought we'd never achieve."

I dropped my hand, the sword resting against my thigh. "I hate that you all are putting your hopes on me. I've done nothing but make mistake after mistake."

Dale smiled. "You have invited us into your territory, you have provided for us, and you are fighting for us. If that isn't a leader, I don't know what is."

Billy Bob seemed to consider Dale's words for a moment, then he looked at me. "He's right. You have done everything a leader would do. Maybe there is a bigger plan."

I raised my brows hopefully. "Did you get in touch with you-know-who?"

He frowned deep enough to crease his brow. "No. But let the tribe try to help. It's an old way, but it doesn't mean it won't work."

"What do I do?" I asked.

Dale shrugged. "I saw it once when I was a boy. I felt the pull of power from our leader before William challenged him the *lupiduci* and emerged victorious. I've never felt it since. I don't think William had enough belief to make the tribal magic work."

"Well, that sounds easy-peasy," I said.

Sunny walked over and held out her hand. "I'll help you," she said. "If I can." She had used her psychic ability to show me the *aether*, the place where Brother Wolf existed.

He'd called her a *seer* as he'd allowed me to glimpse the way he saw our world. We'd never tried to reach him again like this, but I wanted to be the leader the lycanthropes needed, and I couldn't do that without a little help.

I took Sunny's hand. "Let's see if we can find his field again."

"Think about him, like before."

It was hard not to go back to the first place I'd heard his voice. That awful cage. His words of comfort, of support, they had been the only thing to keep me going when I would have otherwise prayed to die.

All will be well, little sister. Hold on. He'd told me that over and over. I'd thought it was my own fractured psyche speaking to me, but when he'd materialized in Billy Bob's guest bedroom as a shadowy figure, I'd found out I wasn't crazy, just stalked by a wolf deity.

I closed my eyes and inhaled deeply, and I smelled fresh green grass as my brown December field transformed into a magical pasture. The one Brother Wolf had taken me to the only other time Sunny had acted as a conduit.

A man with deep caramel skin and hair as dark as pitch stood with his back to me. I approached, realizing I was on four legs, not two. I was wolf again.

"Little sister," the man said. When he turned his awe-inspiring gaze on me, his eyes were as dark as his hair and the pupil-less orbs seemed to hold a million stars. "Why have you come?"

"Because you haven't been returning my calls," I said, which was weird considering I had a muzzle.

"I've been busy with other concerns," he told me.

"Well, I know you told me once that time is not fluid here, and that you see the past, the present, and the future as if it is all happening at once."

"It is," he said as if I were a child. "There is nothing that has or will happen that isn't happening now."

"That's wonderful for you, but for me, in the *non-aether,* you know, down on earth. Shit is happening in a linear fashion, and I'm afraid I'm going to royally screw everything up."

He gave me a disapproving look as the stars in his eyes began to swirl. "And what would you have of me, child? I can guide, but I cannot do."

I trotted up to him and sat at his feet. "You've been a little lackadaisical in the guidance department of late."

"Are you calling me lazy?"

Okay, I'd probably gone too far with my last remark, but come on. "Look, first you send all those lycanthropes at us without any warning, and now that I have to fight some stupid ritual battle for leadership of the tribe, you have completely flaked."

"First, I did not send them to you. They are there because they asked for help, and I showed them another way.

They chose to come to you. Second, you do not need me for the battle ahead. You are well-equipped."

"Have you seen me fight?" I asked. "I'm a hot mess with or without a sword."

"Goodbye, little sister," Brother Wolf said. "We will speak again." He reached down and tapped my forehead.

When I opened my eyes, I was on the ground next to Sunny. Billy Bob knelt beside me, and Willy stayed close to Sunny, who once again had a bloody nose. When she opened her eyes, they were bloodshot as if someone had tried to strangle her.

Damn it. I'd forgot that the current visions had been taking such a physical toll on her.

She finally opened her eyes and moaned as she rolled to her side. Willy held a handkerchief, probably Billy Bob's, to Sunny's nose.

"Are you okay?" I asked her.

"Well, dat was weird," she said.

"Did you see the field?" I asked.

"Dno," she said, unable to make clear "no" with her nose plugged. "I diddit see anything."

"Then what was weird?"

"I'll tell you later," she said.

Willy and Billy Bob help Sunny and me to our feet. "You

take care of Sunny," I told him. If I wasn't going to get any help from Brother Wolf, I was going to have to get seriously better with the sword on my own.

Before Billy Bob could take her away, Sunny put her hand on my shoulder. "Let down the walls, Chav. It's the only way to let them in."

Five hours later, I was still no better with the sword, and I hadn't been able to take any super powers from the lycans. Tomorrow was D-day, and at this rate, it was going to take a massive miracle to save the werewolves, myself, and my wedding night.

CHAPTER TEN

ecember 21st, either the best night of my life or the worst. The outcome remains to be seen...

"The weather man is a liar, liar, pants on fire," I told Sunny as she pushed me into Babe's four-wheel drive SUV in two feet of snow, big flakes coming down all around us. "This is not the unseasonable warm temperatures you promised."

"You know you wanted a white wedding, so yay! You got it. I even made sure there were plenty of red rose petals for Baby Jude to sprinkle down the aisle ahead of you."

I'd put on my parka, scarves, and gloves, thankful that we'd dropped the dress and shoes off with Mary Jane Adams earlier in the week. "I wanted a white wedding before I knew I was going to have to have a cage match right before the ceremony."

"It'll clear up before the wedding," she said with forced optimism. "No worries. We'll figure it out. I promise."

"Unless you saw it in a vision, I am not buying it." It was already noon, sunset was at four-twenty-three, the exact time for the solstice sunset. We would have said our "I dos" just as the sun dipped under the horizon. Now, I was going to have to fight my husband-to-be's daughter during my magical timeline, and unless I made quick work of her or she of me, I was going to miss it all together. "I'll be married no matter what happens, right?"

Sunny, two-handing the wheel, nodded her head. "Uh huh. Son-of-a-gun, it's coming down out here. It's a good thing I got all your wolfies over to the Adams' farm this morning. With the blizzard, Mary Jane is going to need all the help she can get to finish the set up.

Sunny, in standard Sunny-fare, had enlisted Willy, Ruth, Jo Jo, Dakota, and the lycanthropes to help with snow removal. The way she delegated, she should have been the leader of wolves, not me. Unfortunately, her human-ness disqualified her from the job.

Mary Jane Adams had been renting out her beautiful farm house, barn, and immaculately landscaped grounds for proms, weddings, and other events for years, so she probably had a contingency plan. At least I hoped so. But still, I felt a little better knowing, she had extra help. Billy Bob and I had chosen to get married at the gazebo by the lake, but I wasn't sure how that was going to work out if the wedding aisle was under several feet of snow and ice.

It took us forty minutes to get there, an extra thirty minutes because of the treacherous roads, but we'd finally made it. Sunny ushered me inside the farmhouse and right up to the bridal suite and stayed to help me with all my bridal needs. But as I'd told her, if she couldn't magically make me Zorro, I wasn't sure how much she could help. Doc and I had slept in separate rooms the night before, and I'd escaped the house without him seeing me. I mean, not to be too super-stitious, but this wedding had enough problems without breaking all the tried and true traditions as well.

Although, he'd see me at the fight, so my quest for wedding traditions seemed futile, and frankly, stupid. "I wish Billy Bob were here."

"Tough," Sunny said. "What are you wearing to the fight? And have you decided where it will be? I mean, there is the big horse corral by the barn. That's a good location."

"I'm already at a disadvantage," I said. "I don't think trying to slog through the snow "while dodging Etta's swings is a good idea."

"Gotcha," she said. "There's still time to elope."

Eloping was sounding more and more like a reasonable plan. But could I run away with thirty-six lycanthropes in tow? Probably not. I hated that my biggest worry should be whether I tripped over my heels on the way down the aisle, but instead, I had weather, and a vendetta to contend with. It was all Billy Bob's father's fault. That man needed a good thrashing.

"Maybe we could hire someone take out William Smith," Sunny said as if reading my mind. "That would solve half your problems."

"Could we?" I asked.

We both shook our heads. "Therianthropic law is pretty harsh when it comes to things like killing people. Even jerks like William." She wet locks of my hair and wrapped them around sponge curlers. "But maybe we could set up some delays. If he and Etta arrived late, maybe they would lose by default."

"I don't think it works that way."

It does not, Brother Wolf said. *Do not hinder what must happen.*

"I felt that," Sunny said. "I guess your Spirit Wolfy in the Sky says no."

"You guess right." I missed the days when he was telling me all would be well. Where were those words of encouragement now?

"It'll all work out one way or the other," Sunny said, rolling another curl.

"That's not comforting." I patted one of the rollers in my hair. "You know this is just going to get ruined by the fight."

"Maybe not. After all, it's a sword fight not a wrestling match. And this way, there will be less to do to get you gorgeous for the ceremony." She wrapped another one. "Not that you need much help."

Ruth knocked outside of the Bridal Suite door. "William and Etta have arrived."

"Craptastic," I said. "How in the world am I supposed to fight her in this weather?"

"Willy and some of the lycans cleared a spot in the reception tent. Mary Jane had had it put up yesterday, so the ground inside is clear of snow." She wore her worry like a coat. "Why are you doing this, Chavvah? This isn't your fight?"

Oh, how I wished that were true. "It is now, Ruth." I met her gaze. "Are you with me?"

"Of course," she said. "We all are."

SUNNY DID my face up with waterproof, smudge-proof, pretty much destruction-proof make up, and wrapped my curler laden hair that she'd heated with a blow dryer, with cling wrap to protect all her hard work. I'd protested a little, but Sunny had insisted that it was the only way to make sure my hair was fresh and lovely for the ceremony. Willy and Ruth had set up a small dressing area at the back of the tent, where I could shimmy into my dress, as long as I was still alive, and they could add the finishing touches before they raced me down the aisle to marry Billy Bob.

It was four o'clock in the afternoon when we started our trek to the reception tent. There were a ton of vehicles parked out by the barn, but I didn't see many people, and as we reached our destination, I figured out why. All of our guests, nearly two hundred people, including the lycans, William and Etta, and my mate were waiting inside crowded around the edges, leaving a small clearing in the middle.

My father stood next to my mom, and he looked scared and anxious. Mom looked furious, but she was smart enough to hold her tongue.

"I had Willy tell her we'd have the werewolves throw her out on her ass if she made so much as a peep," Sunny whispered in my ear.

I gave my BFF a grateful smile. Just inside, Billy Bob, standing next to Brady, Ed, and Babel, his three grooms-man, wore the white tuxedo I'd chosen with silver lapels. Hot damn, my guy was sex on a stick! Hubba.

William and Etta walked out into the cleared center. The lycanthropes were expectedly nervous, but the theri-anthropes, who had no stake in the outcomes, were understandably curious about the strange pre-wedding show.

I stepped forward the center. My father disengaged from my mother and met me there. "What are you doing, honey?"

"I'm solving a little family crisis, Dad."

"Your mother and I are worried about you."

"I appreciate the concern, but I'm okay."

He looked around the room at the crowd, which was starting to move in around us for a closer look. "It doesn't seem like you're okay."

"Then you haven't been paying attention." I looked up at him and allowed my wolf to surface a little, knowing that my blue eyes would turn golden-yellow. "I am no longer just one thing." I gazed out at our friends and the lycans, a sense of calm settling over me. "I am many. And I am needed."

He nodded, and I could see he was trying to accept what I'd told him, but he also looked a little afraid. Maybe for me. Maybe of me. I wasn't sure.

"It's okay, Dad. I'm afraid, too, but not for the same reasons. I'm afraid to fail, because if I fail, I don't just fail myself, I fail all of them."

He leaned over and kissed my cheek. "Then don't fail," he said. "Win."

William, in the fashion of someone who thinks the sun and moon rises on his ass, took the floor. "If I can have your attention," he demanded. "I am here to seek justice for my tribe. He gestured toward the group of lycan-thropes. My people, who have been stolen from me. I demand satisfaction under the lycanthropic law, by rite of *lupiduci.* There were a few murmurs of dissatisfaction from the werewolves, but the therians were quietly hanging on his every word. This was a glimpse into another world for them, and they didn't want to miss a second of it. "I call Etta Lynn Smith as my second, and as by my right, my champion. Will William Robert Smith, Junior, name a second?"

William already knew I was going to fight Etta, so this part was complete showboating for the town. Was he trying to shame Billy Bob into fighting Etta instead? That seemed silly, considering she had a much better shot against me.

Etta stared across the room at Billy Bob, waiting for his response. It dawned on me then, that William was once again playing a game, but I wasn't sure who he was trying to manipulate more, Etta or his son.

"Chavvah Adine Trimmel will be my champion," Billy Bob said. "It will be a fight to first blood only." Many in the crowd gasped. I guess word hadn't gotten around to everyone about the pre-wedding rumble. They'd probably just followed the smaller groups into the tent out of curiosity. Billy Bob walked over to me and handed me a sword. This one had a deep azure leather grip, the pommel was silver-casted full moon, and the quillon, the part that stopped your hand from sliding up the blade, was two carved wolf heads. The blade was sharp and thin, but longer than the one I'd practiced with.

"Where did you get this?" I asked.

"It's mine," my mate said. "Inherited from my grandfather. I never thought it would be used though."

The love that I saw in his face when he looked down at me rallied my courage. "I can't wait to marry you."

"Then hurry up," he said, "so we can get on with it." He kissed me. "I am with you."

The werewolves in chorus added, "We are with you."

William cleared his throat, and once again took the spotlight. "In one minute, the sun will start to set, and the solstice will begin. On that mark, the two champions will fight. First blood wins. And when Etta is victorious, the lycanthropes of White Rock must leave the area immediately to either return home or face the shunning."

"This is intense," I heard someone say.

I agreed.

Sid Taylor, our officiate and the sheriff of Peculiar, stepped up next to Billy Bob and cleared his throat. "I've been told of the terms of this ritual." He gave a warning look at Etta and William. "If more than first blood is spilled here today, I won't hesitate to arrest whoever crosses the line."

He gave me a look that said I was included in the warning then gave me an encouraging nod. "It's your show, Chavvah."

I nodded back. To my foes, I added, "I have terms as well.

If I win, William will depart immediately, never to return to Missouri." I looked at Etta. "While, Etta, as Billy Bob's daughter, and by right, mine, once we are married, may choose to stay if she wishes, and live here under our protection."

Another gasp went through the crowd, but I couldn't tell if it was because I'd outed Etta as Billy Bob's daughter or if it was because I said she could stay. It was probably both.

William's expression soured. He nodded his head. "Agreed." A loud *BING* silenced the crowd. William held out his phone, the timer visible. "It has begun," he said.

Etta lunged at me, wasting no time trying to draw first blood. I managed to side step her thrust before it made contact with my arm. She swung again in an arc, and I dove, rolling on my shoulder to keep the curlers from digging into my scalp. Wowza, she was fast. I'd barely rolled up to my feet when she began slicing and dicing in my direction.

Let down the wall.

That's what Sunny had said the night before after her vision.

Let them in.

I don't know how.

I threw up my arm and blocked Etta's blow with my

sword. She dropped down and swept my feet with her leg, and I ended up rolling to avoid her steel scraping my calf. Man, this girl was relentless, and definitely in a different class than I was when it came to fighting. So, why hadn't she tagged me, yet. By all accounts, she should have struck first blood in the first seconds, but she kept missing. How was it possible?

Let down the wall. This time the words took the voice of Brother Wolf. *It is time, little sister. Let them in.*

I'd spent so much time keeping my guard up, trying not to let anyone see how damaged I was inside, and how much it hurt that I couldn't have a child. Not wanting Billy Bob to know the depths of my pain. I think I'd resurrected the walls so high it was going to take a wrecking ball and a truck load of dynamite to take it down.

You have children, Chav. These lycans are yours to care for. Do not grieve. Rejoice in your abundance.

I stood up and retreated toward the back of the tent to give myself some room to breathe, but Etta was right on me, so light and agile. I reached out to the wolves, to my mate, to my community. *Help me*, I pleaded silently as I parried when she thrusted, and pivoted when she shed my sword from her to avoid her next attack. I sought with my mind, trying to feel the room of people, trying to open myself to the possibility.

Do not try, Brother Wolf said. *Do.*

When did you turn in to Yoda?

Duck.

I ducked. And then, I stopped trying and I did. As I spun away from Etta, I dropped all my shields, and the pain of my past bubbled inside me like a molten tarpit, threatening to pull me down until I disappeared. But in the pain, I also felt something new. Love. Lots of love. Strength. Power. And also, hope. I latched on to those feelings, as my sight blurred under my tears.

It didn't matter. With the support of our people, their belief in me, I was invincible. When Etta swung across at me, I leapt into the air, high over her head, and with the barest flicker of my blade, I nicked her right shoulder.

A tiny bit of blood welled to the surface. A roar of cheer rippled through the crowd as Etta took a knee in defeat.

"I'm sorry, Father," she said to William. "I have failed you, but I will not leave you if you command it."

"You're worthless!" He lifted her from the ground and threw her into one of the tables. My wedding cake toppled over into her lap, and as she tried to scoop it away, tears spilled down her cheeks and the red raspberry filling covered her hands.

Like blood, I thought. *Like Sunny's prediction.*

"Get up!" William shouted. "Get up and let's go."

"*Enough!*" A voice that was not my own poured from my lips in a booming timber. "*You shall submit, lupin princept.*"

William's looked away for a second, startled, but recovered quickly. "Who are you to command me?"

"This one that I speak through knows me as Brother Wolf. You know me as *Lykaondrea.*" I didn't feel my body shift, but as my eyeline raised, I knew that Brother Wolf was, once again, using me as his avatar. He'd turned me into a ginormously huge black wolf in the blink of an eye. It wasn't the first time Brother Wolf had used me to communicate with this earthly plane, but it didn't mean I liked it. However, this time, because it was to take on William, I wouldn't complain.

Just don't mess up my make up, I told him. *Or my hair. Sunny will never forgive either of us. And make it quick. I have a wedding to get to.*

"Forgive me, little sister, but this petulant wolf will know his place," he said this out loud. Out of the corner of my eye, I saw my mom and dad had taken several steps back, along with almost everyone else in the tent.

But William Smith was a different kind of stubborn. He actually took a step toward me. *Please, Brother Wolf*, I pleaded. *Please don't eat my soon to be father-in-law even if he is the biggest douchebag on earth. Not on my wedding day.*

Billy Bob stood next to us. "Brother Wolf," he said reverently. "I know it is tempting to kill my father, but I request you let him live at this time as long as he leaves immediately."

"I do not like him," Brother Wolf said. *"He is…"*

A dick, I offered.

I felt my huge black head go full emphatic nod. "*Yes, little wolf, he is a dick.*"

Billy Bob's eyes widened.

Brother Wolf snapped his jaws, effectively shutting William up.

The jaw snapping was you, little sister. We have his attention, now. You may finish what needs to be done.

When Brother Wolf gave me back my body, I stared down William Smith until he cowered. What I said next, seemed to come out of nowhere. At least, nowhere I could explain. "I am *spiritus princeptis, bearer of the flame, keeper of the word, and protector of those who accept my protection. You, William Smith, shall leave now and never return.*"

I looked at Etta, who'd finally found her feet with Billy Bob and Jo Jo's help.

"Do you wish to stay, Etta? You have a place here. A home. I would be proud to call you daughter," Billy Bob said.

I nodded. "Me too."

Etta gave William a quick glance then nodded. "I received the call as well. The dream was given to us all. I will stay as is the will of Brother Wolf." To William, she said, "Goodbye, Father."

The elder werewolf roared his frustration, but in the face of over two hundred adversaries, he fled the tent.

"All right," Sunny said, clapping her hands. "Let's get this wedding going. Everybody to the gazebo. The bride will be there in two minutes!" And before the tent could empty, Willy and Ruth had already yanked my shirt over my head and the plastic bag off my curlers.

CHAPTER ELEVEN

I ditched the snow-boots for closed-toed satin and lace heels under my wedding dress. They were decadent and completely impractical for a winter wedding, but I had to trust that the path to the lake had been cleared for me. Sunny, Ruth, and Willy finally stopped fussing over my attire to take a gander at their handiwork.

"You look so beautiful," Sunny said as she fluffed the loose curls. She reached into a small bag and pulled out a white box.

"What's this?" I asked when she handed it to me.

"You have to have something new," she said.

I opened the box to find a small white-gold hair clip with interlocking cubes. "It's lovely."

"It's an endless knot," Sunny said. She took the clip from

me and put it in my hair. "As you know, I grew up with teachings from all kinds of different cultures and philosophies."

"In the cult."

"Compound," she corrected with a smile. "Anyhow. One of my favorite symbols was the Buddhist endless knot. It stands for eternal love and friendship and how one can't exist without the other. That's us, my love. Eternal friends. But it's also you and the doc. He loves the shit out of you, and it's about time the two of you tied the knot for good." She held me out to get a final look. "Aww, honey." She used a tissue to dab beneath my eyes to catch my tears. She put down the tissue. "Perfect," she said. "I told you this make up would hold up."

"I love your guts, Sunny."

"Back at ya," she said.

Ruth handed me a small blue silk square with scalloped edges and a fancy C.A.S embroidered in the center. "Tuck this into your top," she said. "Your something blue."

"You guys," I told them, working hard to hold it together.

Then it was Willy's turn. "I had something for your something borrowed, but your mom gave me these diamond earrings for you to wear. She said she wore them on her wedding night." Willy handed me the pair. They were a half carat each, and I'd seen my mom where them at special occasions more than once over the years. "She said they are your something old and something borrowed."

I put them on, feeling more kindly toward my mom than I had in a long time, and a little guilty for the way I'd been treating her, which had probably been her intention.

"Are you ready?" Sunny asked.

I'd never felt so ready for anything in all my life. "Yes. Let's do this."

The three of us hugged briefly, then I ushered them out in front of me.

When it was my turn to step outside, snowflakes fell over my shoulders and they sparkled against the crimson colored sky. My father waited for me outside the tent.

He took my arm as I stood next to him. "You're beautiful, honey."

"Thanks, Dad." A week ago, I hadn't wanted my parents at the wedding, and now, I couldn't imagine this moment without them.

Sunny, Willy, and Ruth scooted in front of us. They were joined by Babel, Brady, and Ed. Over loud speakers, *Going to the Chapel* by The Dixie Cups began the processional, and I could hear the giggles and laughter that it was meant to evoke. I couldn't see Billy Bob inside the gazebo, and I was anxious to get down there. I had to wait, though, for the bridesmaids and the groomsmen to make their way to the end of the aisle. After the wedding party made it down, Michele Thompson held Jude's hand as they walked down the white runner leading to the lake, as my adorable nephew threw red petals over the ground.

At one point, he put the basket on his head, dumping the entire contents over him. The guests laughed more as Michele scooped up what she could before they completed their mission. When they were done, *At Last* by Etta James, began to play.

We'd picked the song because it was not only true, our love had finally come along, but also because Etta James had the same name as Billy Bob's mom. It had been a way to incorporate her into our day. Of course, we hadn't known about his daughter Etta when we'd made the decision, but it didn't matter. It was our song, and it was beautiful.

I patted Dad's hand. "That's our cue," I said. We walked with measured pace down the aisle as all our friends and family stood up to watch. Jean Taylor was dabbing at tears as we passed by, and she wasn't the only one. It was almost dark now, which meant we'd missed our window to finish the ceremony with the setting sun, but I didn't care. It was finally happening. I was finally marrying the love of my life. At last.

When we were about thirty feet from the gazebo, I saw him. Billy Bob stood facing me. I couldn't stop the tears as I met his loving gaze. Thank heavens for Sunny and her indestructible make up job. Sid Taylor, acting as our officiant, was positioned in the center of the circular dome toward the back. Sunny and the girls were glassy eyed with unshed tears, and I prayed they would hold it together or the four of us would be puddles before I reached my destination.

My mother handed me a bouquet of white and red roses laced with baby's breath when we reached the end of the aisle.

I mouthed the words, "Thank you," as I tugged at my earlobe.

She nodded and smiled.

I turned my attention back to my groom. Billy Bob looked so handsome, and with the emotion on his face, I nearly lost it right then and there. Instead, I let loose a maniacal giggle that sent a titter of laughter through the guests. Billy Bob grinned at me.

Sid stepped forward and asked, "Who presents this woman as she joins her soul to another in partnership to begin on a life long journey of love and adventure?"

My father led me up the steps and placed my hand in Billy Bob's. "Her mother and I do."

I glanced back at my mom. She nodded, blinking back the tears as she covered her mouth with her hand. I knew she loved me, even if she was overbearing ninety percent of the time and drove me crazy. After seeing Billy Bob's only parent in action, I had a new appreciation for my own.

I joined Billy Bob up on the stage, and I couldn't take my eyes off his gorgeous face. He'd shaved and wore his hair loose the way I liked it.

"I love you," he said.

"I love you," I told him back.

Sid said, "Are you both ready?"

"Yes," we both said quickly and simultaneously. The crowd laughed again. I was glad we could amuse them, but frankly, I worried that if we didn't get on with it, someone would snatch the moment away.

"Friends and family, we are gathered here today, to celebrate the love and union of two people who I have the privilege and pride to call my friends. Billy Bob Smith and Chavvah Adine Trimmel, did not arrive at this moment easy. However, they have arrived together, and they have been unwavering in their commitment to each other. Rarely do you come upon two people who couldn't be more different, but whom fit together like two puzzle pieces that complete a picture." Sid smiled at us. "I am honored to officiate their joining, and if anyone can see any cause why these two should not be married, speak now or forever hold your peace."

I held my breath, ready to attack anyone who so much as coughed. The guests remained silent. I let out a small sigh of relief. Billy Bob shook his head at me and smiled.

Sid, who looked as relieved as I was, smiled as well. "The happy couple have both written their own vows. Billy Bob, if you would like to start first..."

Billy Bob nodded. "Chav," he said, his voice choked with emotion. He cleared his throat and continued. "Until you came along, I never knew what it meant to really love someone. I am unworthy of you, as all men would be unworthy. You are my best friend, my lover, my confidant.

I love you down to my very soul, and I will spend every day of the rest of our lives showing you how grateful I am that you chose to love me back. You are the stars to my darkest skies, lighting the way and leading me home. I make this promise, today in front of our closest friends and family, that I will remain unfailingly faithful and devoted to you and those you hold dear. If you fall, I will catch you. If you suffer, I will ease you. If you are vulnerable, I will protect you." Billy Bob took my wedding band from Babe and slid it onto my left ring finger. His expression became very serious as he said, "From this day forward, all that I am, all that I have to offer, it is yours. I am yours."

A noisy sob escaped me. My hands trembled, and he held them to his chest, already giving me the support he'd just promised. I steadied my breath and spoke from my heart.

"Billy Bob, I was lost, and you found me. I was broken, and you healed me. I was unable to love until you loved me. I never expected to find someone who would put me first. Who would love me unconditionally. Imagine my surprise," I said with a hint of a smile, "when that person turned out to be you." Billy Bob chuckled, and the sound turned my smile into a beam that made my cheeks hurt. "I make this promise, today, in front of our closest friends and family, that I will remain unfailingly faithful and devoted to you and those you hold dear. If you fall, I will catch you. If you suffer, I will ease you. If you are vulnerable, I will protect you." I took Billy Bob's wedding band from Sunny and slid it onto his finger. "From this day forward," I said, All that I am, all that I have to offer, it is yours. I am yours."

Sid placed his hand over ours. "By the exchange of rings, you are consenting to be bound together, promising to love and honor each other for the rest of your lives. By the authority vested in me by the Tri-State Council and by the laws of the state of Missouri, I am happy to pronounce you husband and wife." Sid grinned at Billy Bob. "Go ahead, man. Kiss your bride."

'Finally," Billy Bob said as he took me in his arms. The guests cheered as he pressed his mouth against mine and kissed me until I saw stars. "Hello, wife," he said when we came up for air.

"Hello, husband."

Sid then yelled for the crowd, "Ladies and gentlemen, I present to you, Dr. and Mrs. Billy Bob and Chavvah Smith." The guests stood up, clapping as we made our way down the aisle together toward the reception tent. I didn't even feel the cold anymore. It was as if my body refused to feel anything but pure unadulterated happiness.

We danced the night away, our Peculiar friends and our tribe, mingling like old friends until it was time to make our escape.

"I'm the luckiest man in the world," Billy Bob said as he swung me in his arms.

"Good thing you didn't say person," I told him. "I would have you beat."

"Not possible," he said, and then he kissed me like he'd planned to kiss me for the rest of my life.

You have done well, little sister.

I was glad the spirit wolf had shown up. He was a big reason I had a life to share with my guy. *Thanks, Brother Wolf. I couldn't have made it here without you.*

You are much stronger than you know. And your children will be strong because of you.

I saw Sunny doing the two-step with Babe, and remembered I had a small bone to pick with my spirit guide. *Could you please stop damaging Sunny when you send her visions?*

I am not damaging the blonde seer, he said.

What do you call the seizures? The bloody noses? Just knock it off.

I did not injure her. I remade her. For you.

I don't understand. What the heck was Brother Wolf doing to Sunny in my name?

She will age more slowly now, like you. As long as you live, she will live.

Are you serious?

Yes. I see many versions of the future, and the one where you are the most contented is the one where she is in your life. So, I fixed her.

A giggle of disbelief, relief, and sheer joy bubbled up

inside me. Billy Bob moved behind me and wrapped his arms around my waist. "Everything okay?"

I laughed out loud then. "This is truly the happiest day of my life."

ONE MONTH LATER, the honeymoon is still going strong...

"Today's the day," I said to Billy Bob. My hands had been sweaty, and I'd been nauseous with worry all day waiting to hear how the town council would vote on whether our tribe could stay in Peculiar or not. There had been several voices of dissent in town, but also a few supporters. I'd been allowed to speak and reminded the good folk that many of us came to town as outsiders, but it didn't make us dangerous and undesirable. And anytime someone would say, "But lycanthropes...," Doc would happily remind them that he was a lycan and that hadn't prevented him from delivering their babies or taking care of them when they were sick. His contribution to this town as a doctor and a spiritual leader had done the most to shut up the naysayers. Still, it would come down to today's behind closed door vote.

"When did Babel say he would call?" Billy Bob asked.

"As soon as he had a verdict." The town council was comprised of Babel, because he was the mayor, Blondina Messer, Ed Thompson, Sid Taylor, Delbert Johnson, and Robbin Clubb. If the vote wasn't unanimous, they could turn down our request, and I had no idea where Blondina or Robbin stood on the matter. I could only hope the vote would fall our way.

We'd celebrated Christmas and New Years with the lycan-thropes, and we'd offer to let Etta move into the house with us, but she decided to stay in tent city with the other werewolves. She has a lot of anger to overcome, so we didn't push her. Also, I told Sunny about what Brother Wolf had been doing to her body. She made me promise to give him a giant smooch for her if I was given the opportunity. Babel said to give him one for him as well. However, Billy Bob said I wasn't allowed to give anyone smooches but him. I was okay with that.

But now, my stomach roiled with anticipation. "They need to call before I yark all over the place. I can't believe how sick I feel right now." Really, I hadn't felt good in a week. "This situation has got my stomach upset. That, on top of the bloating, is about to do me in."

Billy Bob gave me a strange look. "When do you feel sick?"

"Mornings mostly but sometimes the afternoon, like now. Why? Is there a flu going around? Damn it, I can't get sick right now. There is too much to do."

"Are you feeling more tired than usual?"

"Yes. A lot. I found myself nodding off in the back office after I closed Sunny's Outlook the other night."

"Are your breasts tender?"

I reached up and felt them. "A little," I said suspiciously.

"And when was your last period?"

"No," I told him. "It's not possible. We both know it." The phone rang. I picked it up. "I'll have to call you back."

"Wait!" Babel said. "The town council has made their decision. The lycanthropes can stay for a probationary period of one year, if after that time they have successfully integrated into Peculiar as productive citizens, they can become permanent residents."

"Thanks," I said numbly and hung up. "The tribe can stay."

"When was your last period, Chav?"

I did the math, counting back to before our wedding. "Six weeks ago," I said. "But the damage..."

Billy Bob gathered me close, inhaling my scent deeply. "I can smell the difference. I think I've been smelling the pregnancy for weeks now, but my instinct couldn't reconcile what my brain thought it knew to be absolute."

"Don't get your hopes up. Not until we do the test."

"I have a stack of them in my office," he said. "Can you pee?"

"Can I? Of course, I've been going so often I was worried I had a bladder infection."

Three minutes later, I'd peed on a stick, and we waited for what I really believed would be a disappointing minus.

It was a plus.

"Baby," Billy Bob said. He cupped my face between his hands and kissed me enthusiastically. "You're having our baby."

My hands began to shake so badly, I dropped the test on the ground. "I don't understand."

I see all your futures, little sister. In this one, you are the most happy.

"So, you fixed me," I said. Like he'd fixed Sunny.

"What?" Billy Bob asked.

"It's a gift," I said. "We've been given a gift." And I couldn't wait to tell Sunny all about it.

The End

Madder Than Hell Book 1

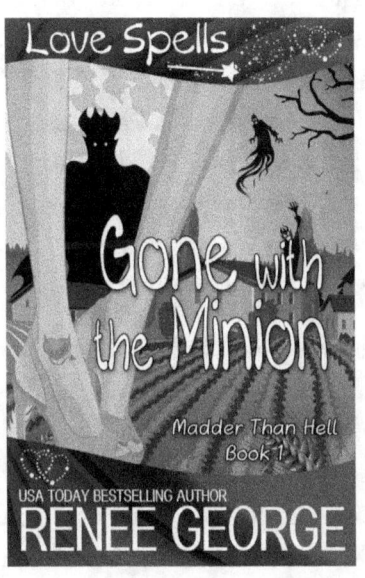

How do you save your family when they're about to lose the literal farm? You make a deal with a demon, of course. And then you spend the next one

hundred and forty-nine years making him sorry he forced you to sign in blood on the dotted line.

To save her family, Southern Belle Olivia "Liv" Madder made a bargain with a demon lord and ever since, she's been haunted...by her three dead sisters, and her own guilty conscience. Every decade, since the deal, Liv has had to find a human willing to bargain their soul with Moloch. If she fails, even once, he'll not only drag her to Hell, but he'll take her sisters, too. It doesn't mean she can't make Lord Jerkface miserable in the process by removing his lesser demons from the Earthly plane.

When her latest contracted soul dies before the bargain is sealed, she has less than four days to find another soul or her own agreement will be broken. But Moloch offers her a get-out-of-Hell-free card: steal an old book once owned by paranormal researcher David Jensen. The same David Jensen she fell in love with sixty years ago but left to protect him and his family. Then Moloch drops the biggest bombshell: David has died.

Heartbroken and feeling she has no choice, Liv makes the trip to Sanctum, Missouri only to find David's grandson has the book. Worse, he's keeping a mysterious family secret that threatens Moloch, Liv, and her three sisters. What's a minion to do when her world falls apart? Get Madder than Hell and kick some demon butt.

Available at All Your Favorite eTailers

Chapter One

It took me two seconds to spot my mark and about half that time for him to spot me. He was on the move. Right out the opened French doors. I could see he was headed toward the garden. Why, oh, why did they always run? I shoved my way through the crowd of monkey suits and silk chiffons with as much grace as I could muster. Not an easy feat considering I was stuffed into the ill-fitting, scarlet-red, mermaid-cut, satin dress I'd...um, borrowed from the unconscious woman in the coat room. A frock more billowy and less mermaid-y would've been a better choice for running, but I'd picked this one because it matched my red stiletto pumps and my patent-leather clutch with its removable silver chain. The little purse hung off my shoulder and slapped against my thigh as I wiggled through the crowd.

I finally made it outside. Freshly blossomed lilacs burst out from the multitude of bushes like tufts of purple cotton candy and sweetened the humid air. I looked over my shoulder and saw that no one noticed, or more likely, cared that I was chasing the party's host into the lavish garden.

The three-story mansion was overly ostentatious, even for Jefferson City, the capital of Missouri. The monstrosity, with its marble columns and wrought-iron balconies, reminded me of the plantation a few miles from my father's modest farm in Georgia, where I'd been born and raised. In other words, the place stuck out like a bedazzled T-shirt at a Sunday morning church service. The owner of the mansion, Carmine Hennessy, was a lobbyist for some major companies in the northwest area of the state, and he was holding a fundraiser for his clients. Also, he wasn't human—at least not completely—which made him an excellent fit for politics.

"Stop right there!" I screamed after the fiend. I watched him hightail it around the corner of the eight-foot-high hedge that surrounded the ornamental grounds. Good. The partygoers wouldn't see me take ol' Hennessey down. Bless the face-melting heat of the Missouri summer—no one inside would venture outside lest common sweat ruin their designer duds.

Unlike my attire, the lobbyist's tailored tuxedo was perfect for hauling ass. The tight red evening dress hugged my knees and made it hard to do much but waddle like a penguin. I tottered around the shrubbery and took an awkward step forward. My heel dipped sideways, and the dewed grass kissed the side of my foot. Ack! My heels! My dearly departed sister Charlotte would be appalled at the treatment of my footwear.

I saw my target just a few feet away from another turn in the boxed hedge. I had scoped out the whole area the day before, so I knew the landscape. I also knew I couldn't catch him before he entered the maze surrounding the marble inlay fountain with its ode to Hennessy himself. Yeah. There was a bronze statue of him holding an American flag in one hand and a champagne bottle in the other.

"I just want to talk," I lied. "Don't you want to make a deal?"

Offering to make a deal to a demon was the equivalent of showering a chocolate addict with truffles. He stopped about twenty feet from me and turned back, his head hitching to one side. "So," he sniffed. "You're the Madder. You don't look like much."

I smoothed my dress, and lifted my chin, and poured on my best Southern drawl. "That's just a mean thing to say, sir. Especially to a lady." My "a"s sounded like "uh"s, and I dropped the "r" in sir. I was pretty proud of the fact that I'd managed to master the non-regional American dialect over the years, but every once in a while, it was fun to pull out the Southern Belle.

The demon in the Hennessey suit snorted, the fear draining from his blue eyes. "Frankly my dear, I don't give a damn."

I loved when they underestimated me. But I hated when they quoted *Gone With the Wind*. I dropped the accent. "I'm not Scarlett, and you're for damn sure not Rhett, so let's cut the shit."

He raised a brow. "You know, now that I see you, I don't know what all the hoopla's about." Curling his lip, he sized me up. "You're kind of doughy."

"That hurts." Actually, it did. I don't care how old you are, women are women everywhere, and none of us want to be thought of as doughy—he might as well have said thick, or hippy, or FAT. Sure, I had curves—some in the wrong places—and my size D breasts were threatening to spill over the top of the borrowed dress, but it didn't give this impostor the right to judge. Especially this skinny, short, pale, and balding imposter about to get his face kicked in.

The "hoop-la" as he called it was the buzz in the underworld about a rogue minion going bat-shit all over demon ass. That rogue would be me, Olivia Madder. Of course, this wasn't the first time I'd been called "the Madder." I've been tracking demons for more than a hundred years and some change. And while I'm not always successful in sending them back to Hell, I had a seventy-seven percent completion rate. Charlotte would've called that bragging, but I called it awesome.

"Tell me about the deal," said Hennessey. "It better be good."

The deal was that I was going to fry him. Now that he had me good and pissed, it was time to teach this uncouth jerk what all the fuss was about. I bent my knee up until I could reach my shoe and nearly fell over as the dress caught on the stiletto. In my struggle to stay upright, the back of the dress ripped at the seam.

Hennessey snorted again. "Had I known that stripping was part of your routine, I might not have been so quick to run."

"Right. You insulted my curves, but now you want to see them?" With the breeze literally at my backside, but infinitely more room to move, I toed off the other shoe so I could get good balance on the balls of my feet.

The demon, undoubtedly baffled, raised a brow. "I don't

turn down any opportunity to view the naked female form. Especially given the deficits of my current abode. So, please, do continue bursting out of your clothes."

I flipped him the bird with my free hand, before using my other hand to fling my beautiful red stiletto at him. He seemed startled to be the target of a Frisbee-ing shoe—so you can imagine his surprise when the spiked heel pierced his left eye. I was surprised, too.

I was aiming for his forehead.

A heel between the eyes wouldn't kill the demon, but it would paralyze him long enough for me to work the spell needed to drive him from this plane of existence.

He howled as he toppled onto the well-manicured blue-grass. After a moment, his howls quieted, and he sat up, slack-jawed, and stared at me with his remaining blue eye.

"You rotten bitch." He pointed to the red shoe protruding from his face. "Do you have any idea how hard this body was to come by? And now you've gone and ruined the freaking eyeball."

"If it's any consolation, I didn't mean to hit you in the eye."

"Apology not accepted." He grabbed the heel and struggled to disengage it from his face. "I'm sending you the bill for the blood on my tuxedo."

I leveled my gaze at the demon — oh, sure, he was in human skin, but you can wrap a pile of dog shit in silk, and it's still dog shit, if you catch my meaning — grabbed my other shoe off the ground and tried to walk as menacingly toward my prey as the constricting dress would allow.

I shouldn't have bothered. Hennessey didn't even notice. In fact, he was too busy with shoe extraction to realize I was now standing right beside him.

"What in the name of Moloch is this fucking thing made of?" he yelled.

Iron dipped in holy water and blessed by a white witch, but I wasn't going to tell him that. I held up the other shoe and clicked the steel tip of the heel. A fan of barbs flicked out in a golf ball sized circle. I hit the tip again, and they retracted. The stilettos were my favorite, albeit least comfortable, weapons in my arsenal.

I grabbed the embedded shoe and told the demon, "Hold still."

He tilted his head to the right to give me better access. "Thanks."

Idiot. It was my stylish footwear protruding from his head, and somehow, he thought I was going to help remove it.

"Try not to damage the rest of the face," he ordered. "It's going to be difficult enough to heal the eyeball."

I lowered my head slightly, put on my sweetest smile, and spoke softly. "Don't you worry, honey," I said as I swung my right arm in an arc, "a mangled face is the least of your problems."

"Wait. What?" He looked up at me just in time to realize my intent. Still smiling, I buried the other heel deep into his forehead. *Thud. Crunch. Squish.*

"You suck," the demon mumbled as his left eyelid froze open and he dropped to the ground.

I knelt next to him and, in a gesture taken straight from the offended Southern Belle handbook, I slapped his bloodied face. "That's for your unkind comments about my appearance." I wiped my soiled hands on the demon's shirt. The rusty scent of blood mixed with the fragrance wafting from the colorful flowers planted along the hedges. Well, that was certainly a metaphor of my life— beautiful horror.

All that was left was to send the gored creature back to Hell — once he told me what I wanted to know.

I'd made friends with an Army interrogator back in the nineties. He told me that when they were trying to find Noriega in Panama, they would grab one of his known associates, a person low on the totem pole and easy to find, and make the guy tell them about the next associate, whom they'd go and find, and make that person tell about another one, and so on until they had the location of the tyrant narrowed down.

My focus was less goal-oriented. I only needed to know where to find my next demon. I didn't give a crap about the boss. He was easy to find but impossible to get rid of, so I had to satisfy myself by dispatching all his lackeys. I relied on a website called DemonsAreAmongUs.com. Its forum was filled with quackery from delusional maniacs who blamed demonic possession for every bad thing in their lives, you know, like their local gas station hiking up the price of super unleaded. Sometimes, though, there would be a post that rang of truth, like the awful one I'd read about the demon Lazul.

Unfortunately, this demon was not Lazul. But he was higher on the pecking order in this particular demonic territory—and he would know where to find the asswipe I really wanted to smite. In Kansas City, Lazul had possessed a young woman who'd committed suicide by overdosing on her antidepressants. She'd been declared dead, and her grieving parents were left alone with the corpse to say their goodbyes. Then the fiend had popped into the corpse, growled obscenities, and yelled, "I am Lazul!" The parents screamed as a demon inhabited their daughter's body. He escaped the hospital before anyone could figure out what was happening.

It was the mom's post, and the particular mentions of rotten-egg smell and glowing red eyes, that sent me after the asshole.

"That's just unsavory," a sweet voice said from behind me, slightly aghast.

"Indeed," another voice agreed, but with more interest than disgust.

"Eww," the final voice mewled. "There's goo leaking from his face."

I rolled my eyes and looked at the three young women now crouched over my shoulder, one brunette, and two blondes — the twins — decked out in full-on bustles and bonnets. Charlotte was more practical than our younger sisters, so her dress was made from pink cotton edged with tiny white flowers. The twins wore pale yellow and lavender chiffon frocks with matching lace gloves and bonnets. Not even death could force my sisters into anything less than their finest attire.

"Go away." I shooed at them. "I'm working."

"Now, Olivia," Char chided, crossing her arms tight against her chest. "Is that any way to greet your sisters?" The way she said sisters, sounded like *sistuhs*.

"Y'all are a distraction I don't need at this moment, Char." I turned the demon's head and held his left eyelid open with my thumb. "Eliza, you probably don't want to watch this."

My youngest sister was squeamish, but mostly because she had an empathic streak a mile wide. Even as a small child on the farm she'd bury dead mice—much to the annoyance of our barn cats that had killed the critters. I imagined that she would've been a social worker or something similar had she lived in this day and age.

I dug my index finger into the demon's unmarred eyeball.

"Olivia!" Eliza screeched, her skirts swishing as she skittered backward.

"I told you not to watch."

She buried her face in her hands. The eye gave a little squeak when I breached the surface, and fluid seeped out. It was yucky, but trust me, I've done worse. After a few seconds of digging, I located the bottom of each heel and clicked the barbs closed.

"You used to be the epitome of social standard, Olivia." Charlotte tisked.

"I used to be a lot of things," I said. I glanced at her. "We all did."

Charlotte's gaze fastened on the shoe as I pulled on it. "Careful!" she chided. "It took forever to fix those heels the last time you yanked them out of a vessel's forehead."

"I remember." Considering, I'd done all the work. "I made sure the barbs are closed this time," I told her.

Charlotte had a knack for fixing things. Even with genteel upbringing, Charlotte had always been at home among the farming equipment, fixing broken plows and taking apart tools to figure out how they worked. Poppa, a widowed father, would send us once a week into town to visit with our Aunt Elizabeth, who tried her best to turn us into delicate Belles, but when we were on the farm, Poppa allowed us the freedom of doing more than just house chores. Eliza became an expert on farm animals, pigs, cows, and the like. While Elise, spent all her time reading medical papers she could borrow from Dr. Beauregard Jenkins, a local surgeon, whom she sometimes volunteered with.

Even so, Charlotte couldn't actually get her hands on mechanical objects, but I could, so she walked me through the building and fixing of my demon-hunting weaponry.

Elise, the older of my twin sisters, crouched down for a closer look at the facial damage. I opened the small red clutch and grabbed the three-inch silver rod. I extracted the heel and replaced it with the rod in the center of the demon's forehead. I wiped ocular fluids, brain, and blood from the stilettos onto the demon's shirt, and then slipped them back on my feet.

"I think he has a melanoma on his forehead," Elise said, pointing to a mole on Hennessy's scalp. "It's rough, uneven in color and shape, and I'm sure he never wears sunscreen." She shook her head. "I saw one that looked just like it on Discovery Medicine."

If Elise had been born in modern times, I had no doubt she would be in medical school on her way to being a doctor. I could wish a thousand times my sisters to have different fates, and it wouldn't change a damned thing. Moloch had made sure of that.

I waved at my siblings. "Okay, shoo. Show's over, nothing to see here. Time to go. Last call. Vamoose. Am-scray even."

"You don't have to be rude," said Elise.

"Actually, I do." My sisters could ignore polite, but rude got their attention. Hooking my arms under the demon's armpits, I dragged him around the next hedge. "I'm busy at the moment. I don't have time for niceties. Sorry." Besides, the demon's master—and mine—would be showing up shortly, and I didn't want my sisters anywhere near the foul creature.

All three of them "hmphed" at the same time, then shimmered from sight. Every time they did that, I felt a lightning strike of guilt. The fact that my sisters were ghosts was in no small measure my fault.

I unhooked the chain from the clutch and formed a small circle on the ground next to the paralyzed body. Like the rod, it was made from silver. Demons had what I thought of as a severe allergy to pure silver. Even though I was a minion, the precious metal only felt warm on my skin. It didn't burn.

I'm not evil. Not yet.

I took matches, a votive candle, an orange spice incense cone, a vial of sea salt, a cigarette, and a tiny bell out of the purse. All the items were necessary to the "casting out the boogeyman" spell. Sure, it had another name, a much more complicated, can't hardly get around all the vowels kind of name, but my former demon-hunting partner had deemed it "casting out the boogeyman" and so, that's what we called it.

The familiar heartache threatened to derail my attention. It had been fifty-six years since I'd said goodbye to David Jensen—and yet, it still felt like yesterday. If you're wondering how long it takes to get over that kind of loss, the answer is never.

I poured salt around the silver chain, then I placed the candle and the cone of incense on the north and south edges respectively, struck a match and lit them both. Lifting the demon's hand, I put it inside the loop.

Ugh. I so didn't like this part. I pulled the rod from Hennessey's forehead. The demon howled with rage and pain, his whole body twisting and jerking, except for the trapped hand. His human face contorted in sheer agony. Like I said, silver was bad ju-ju for the damned, and the sea salt made it impossible for the Hellspawn to eject from its host.

That, along with the gaping holes where his eyes used to be, made me shudder inside, a weakness I refused to show to the monsters.

"Hush now," I said, sitting down next to him and trailing my fingers on his brow. "Or the pin goes back in."

"What do you want, Madder?" he asked through gritted teeth.

After all these years, it was still hard to watch human vessels wither under the spell. Sometimes the demons had a shade attached to them, not a ghost exactly — not like my sisters, more like residual energy repeating its traumatic cycle of death over and over. Especially in the newly possessed.

This body didn't have a shade.

It meant this fiend had taken up residence for at least a couple of decades. Hennessy's shade no longer lingered in this realm. "Tell me where I can find Lazul, and I'll let you go." *To Hell.* The Madder wasn't known for mercy to demonkind, and yet, they seem to always believe I'd let them go back to creating havoc for humans.

"I'd rather claw out *your* eyes," the demon rasped.

"Promises, promises." I tapped the hole in his forehead. "Remember who's in charge."

"Bitch!"

"Wow. I hope you don't kiss your mother with that mouth."

"My mother is Sin and Death, and she will feast on your innards while you roast in pits of eternal fire," he screamed, spittle forming in the corners of his lips.

"I know I'm from the South an' all, but I really don't like barbecue." Ugh. He was being stubborn. More stubborn than the average demon who'd roll on another demon to prevent getting a hangnail, let alone the pain of having his hand surrounded by the equivalent of burning pitch.

The body lurched, the empty orbital sockets seemingly staring at me, and Hennessey's voice took on an unnatural tone. "My master will come for you. In the bowels of Hell, you will burn forever. Tenfold, a palsy will fall upon your soul. Tenfold, you will beg for mercy that will never come. Tenfold—"

"Yeah. I got it. Tenfold." I shook my head. "I've heard it all before, asshole." He wasn't going to give me Lazul. From experience, most demons who talked did so in the first minute. This is what I got for trying to go through the slightly higher-ups in the demonic command chain. They weren't as easily broken. Damn it. I really wanted Lazul. Those traumatized parents deserved to put their daughter to rest properly. An empty coffin in the cold ground would be a shitty reminder that her demon-possessed body was running around doing Moloch knew what.

I picked up the cigarette, struck another match, and lit it. Leaning over, I blew a puff of smoke into the demon's face. Cyanide, a by-product of tobacco processing, was a necessary agent in the spell. It didn't take much, and cigarette smoke was the easiest way to transport the minuscule amount of poison, which is why you'd never catch one of Hell's agents smoking.

"Wait. What is that?" His nose twitched as the toxic wisps traveled into his nostrils.

He couldn't see what I was doing, but he realized what was about to happen. Beneath us, the ground shook as the demon fought to release himself from the body before I did. The thing about the boogeyman ritual was that when I used it to expel demons, they got a one-way ticket to Hell. No return trips. It was one of the more satisfying aspects of sending Moloch's lackeys back to the Pit. Time for the *pièce de résistance*. I rang the small bell. Its faint tinkle was reminiscent of a toddler's giggle.

The body instantly stilled.

The demon was gone.

Okay, so most people might have been expecting something spectacular, like out of *Supernatural*. All black smoke, fire, brimstone, explosions, and drama, but nope, just gone.

I'd expected fireworks the first time I cast a demon out of this plane, so I understand the disappointment.

I repacked my clutch, attached the chain before putting it over my shoulder, and got to my feet. I kicked the vessel's thigh. "Take that, Moloch."

Upon mentioning his name, the demon lord burst into existence in front of me.

Fantastic.

Not.

PARANORMAL MYSTERIES & ROMANCES

By Renee George

Witchin' Impossible Cozy Mysteries

www.witchinimpossible.com

Witchin' Impossible (Book 1)

Rogue Coven (Book 2)

Familiar Protocol (Booke 3)

Mr & Mrs. Shift (Book 4)

Barkside of the Moon Mysteries

www.barksideofthemoonmysteries.com

Pit Perfect Murder (Book 1)

Murder & The Money Pit (Book 2)

The Pit List Murders (Book 3)

Peculiar Mysteries

www.peculiarmysteries.com

You've Got Tail (Book 1) FREE Download

My Furry Valentine (Book 2)

Thank You For Not Shifting (Book 3)

My Hairy Halloween (Book 4)

In the Midnight Howl (Book 5)

My Peculiar Road Trip (Magic & Mayhem) (Book 6)

Furred Lines (Book7)

My Wolfy Wedding (Book 8)

Who Let The Wolves Out? (Book 9)

Madder Than Hell

www.madder-than-hell.com

Gone With The Minion (Book 1)

Devil On A Hot Tin Roof (Book 2)

A Street Car Named Demonic (Book 3)

Hex Drive

https://www.renee-george.com/hex-drive-series

Hex Me, Baby, One More Time (Book 1)

ABOUT THE AUTHOR

I am a USA Today Bestselling author who writes paranormal mysteries and romances because I love all things whodunit, Otherworldly, and weird. Also, I wish my pittie, the adorable Kona Princess Warrior, and my beagle, Josie the Incontinent Princess, could talk. Or at least be more like Scooby-Doo and help me unmask villains at the haunted house up the street.

When I'm not writing about mystery-solving werecougars or the adventures of a hapless psychic living among shapeshifters, I am preyed upon by stray kittens who end up living in my house because I can't say no to those sweet, furry faces. (Someone stop telling them where I live!)

I live in Mid-Missouri with my family and I spend my non-writing time doing really cool stuff...like watching TV and cleaning up dog poop.

Join My Newsletter

Follow Me On Bookbub!